She Was Jealous

Gretchen, always so superior, always in command, was jealous of his little flirtation, he thought. It had actually got under her skin—not an easy thing to do—and was therefore all the more pleasing to him.

But Gretchen's feelings went beyond simple jealousy. Jay served her well, letting her take command but playing his own part with the coolest assurance when the time came for it. Jealousy was dangerous. They couldn't afford indiscretions of any sort. . . .

Other SIGNET Romances You'll Enjoy

☐ **THE SHROUDED WAY by Janet Caird.** A search for sunken treasure and a strange death—and Elizabeth Cranston discovers the key to a mystery which places her love and her life in danger. (#Q5753—95¢)

☐ **SECRET HONEYMOON by Peggy Gaddis.** A bride must choose between the man she married and the man suddenly returned from the past. (#P5586—60¢)

☐ **DESIRE UNDER THE ROSE (Condensed for Modern Readers) by Perry Lindsay.** A talented New York actress who exchanges her career for a new role as the wife of a Southern millionaire finds that he can give her everything—except the man she loves. (#P5585—60¢)

☐ **SYLVIA'S DAUGHTER by Ivy Valdes.** An elderly stranger draws Kate Langley into a tangle of love and hate, scandal and death, and dark family secrets. Could even Philippe—the handsome young man who had captured her heart—free her from this web of bitterness and fear? (#P5584—60¢)

☐ **IN SEARCH OF A NAME by Norah Whittle.** Married to a man who was old enough to be her father, Judith Pumphrey yearned for romantic love. Little did she realize that fate would take a hand in reuniting her with Timothy, the man she had once loved. . . .
(#P5583—60¢)

☐ **KISS A STRANGER by Glenna Finley.** The ancient castle held mystery, danger—and unexpected romance.
(#T5173—75¢)

☐ **INTO THE ARENA by Emma Darby.** A probing novel that searches the hearts of two women in love with the same man. (#T5433—75¢)

THE NEW AMERICAN LIBRARY, INC.,
P.O. Box 999, Bergenfield, New Jersey 07621

Please send me the SIGNET BOOKS I have checked above. I am enclosing $_____(check or money order—no currency or C.O.D.'s). Please include the list price plus 25¢ a copy to cover handling and mailing costs. (Prices and numbers are subject to change without notice.)

Name_____

Address_____

City_____State_____Zip Code_____
Allow at least 3 weeks for delivery

Only Couples Need Apply

by
Doris Miles Disney

A SIGNET BOOK
NEW AMERICAN LIBRARY
TIMES MIRROR

All the characters in this book are fictitious, and any
resemblance to actual persons, living or dead,
is purely coincidental.

COPYRIGHT © 1973 BY DORIS MILES DISNEY

All rights reserved. For information address
Doubleday and Company, Inc., 277 Park Avenue,
New York, New York 10017.

Library of Congress Catalog Card Number: 72-92401

This is an authorized reprint of a hardcover edition
published by Doubleday and Company, Inc.

SIGNET TRADEMARK REG. U.S. PAT. OFF. AND FOREIGN COUNTRIES
REGISTERED TRADEMARK—MARCA REGISTRADA
HECHO EN CHICAGO, U.S.A.

SIGNET, SIGNET CLASSICS, SIGNETTE, MENTOR AND PLUME BOOKS
are published by The New American Library, Inc.,
1301 Avenue of the Americas, New York, New York 10019

FIRST PRINTING, JUNE, 1974

1 2 3 4 5 6 7 8 9

PRINTED IN THE UNITED STATES OF AMERICA

Only Couples Need Apply

1

They bought a copy of the Belmont *Register* soon after it appeared on a newsstand and took it with them to the Paradise Grill, all but empty at three o'clock in the afternoon. They sat down in a booth, ordered dry Rob Roys on the rocks and while waiting to be served, turned to the classified section to see what furnished apartments there were for rent.

Out of several, one immediately caught their eye: *Spacious three-room carriage house apartment. Garage included. Only couples need apply. 485-6341.*

"Carriage house," Jay said. "Must be a big place, lot of grounds, if there used to be a carriage house with it."

"Yes, but let's see what the others are," said Gretchen.

They made a handsome couple studying the rest of the ads, both blond, faces tanned from a winter in the Florida sun. Gretchen was the fairer of the two, hair parted in the middle, falling in a shining mantle below her shoulders. She had beautiful eyes, cool gray, open and candid beneath wide-spaced brows. The proud erect way she held her head, her confident manner came from the knowledge that her exquisite looks drew admiring glances wherever she went.

Jay was a darker blond. He wore his thick straight hair medium long—it suited him. He had classic features, a wide sensual mouth, a quick smile that gave him, on the surface, a disarmingly boyish look. His hazel eyes were fringed with dark lashes. He was a shade above medium height, slim and wiry.

Both wore expensive casual clothes, she a soft blue cashmere sweater and skirt, he a plaid jacket of olive and muted gold with olive green slacks. They looked like people with money to support their leisured appearance. Which they were. Not enough money, not nearly as much as they wanted to have, but enough, at least, for now.

Their drinks were served. No other apartments interested them.

"Might as well find out about the carriage house," Gretchen said, getting a dime from her pocketbook.

She tore the ad out of the newspaper, took it with her to the phone booth in the rear of the room and dialed the number.

"Hello?" a woman's voice answered.

"I'm calling about the apartment you have for rent," Gretchen said.

"Oh." A slight hesitancy. "Someone else just called about it."

Someone had been very fast, thought Gretchen—if it was true.

"Would it still be possible for us to see it later?" she asked. "My husband and I, that is."

"Why yes. Later."

"How much is the rent, please?"

"One hundred and fifty a month, heat, water, and electricity included." A crisp businesslike note came into the voice. "How long would you plan to stay?"

"Several months. Through the summer, at least."

"I see. The last couple had it for almost a year. I'd want references."

Gretchen made no comment on that. The apartment seemed more and more promising. She doubted that other people were looking at it yet. The woman was just being cautious.

"What time today could we see it?" she asked.

"Would five o'clock be convenient for you?"

"Just fine."

"May I have your name, please?"

"Gretchen Addison. Mrs. Jay Addison."

"I'm Mrs. Edward Mercer, 519 Lakeview Avenue. Do you know where it is, Mrs. Addison?"

"Not really. We're new here."

"Well, coming from downtown, take Clifton Street off Main and you'll pick it up, the fourth street to your left. It overlooks the lake just two streets away."

"Oh, now I know where it is. My husband and I were out that way yesterday, just driving around. We'll see you then, Mrs. Mercer, at five o'clock."

Only Couples Need Apply 9

Gretchen hung up and went back to Jay. "It's that nice residential section where we saw all the big houses yesterday," she reported. "It might be just what we're looking for. I wonder if there are lake privileges. I didn't ask. There must be, though."

"Privacy," said Jay. "That comes first of all."

Gretchen sat down to finish her drink. "Why don't we drive past now and see what the place looks like?"

They had no trouble following the route they had taken the day before. Belmont wasn't that big, not more than thirty-odd thousand permanent residents, although summer people swelled the population by a few thousand more during the season.

The city sprawled out around the western half of Indian Maid Lake, the largest in northeastern Connecticut, merging with summer cottages along the wooded eastern shore. Half resort town, half industrial—but with most of its industries tucked away nowadays in landscaped industrial parks—it still had in the middle of the downtown area its original village green, old houses around it meticulously restored for business and professional use. The whole city had a quiet orderly charm that the zoning board worked hard to preserve.

Gretchen and Jay had come upon it by accident a few days ago traveling east on I-84, headed for Maine with tentative plans for finding a place there to spend the summer. It was she who noticed a sign that said BELMONT NEXT EXIT and then, BELMONT EXIT 1 MILE.

It was late afternoon. "Why don't we stop there tonight?" she said. "Remember how I won three hundred on a horse at Belmont before we went to California? It's a lucky name for me. We'll find a good motel, have a good dinner somewhere."

Belmont turned out to be nearly twenty miles from the interstate highway, too far away to attract the passing tourist. There wasn't even a sign to tell them it was on a lake until they reached the outskirts of the city and saw one pointing to it. Presently they came to the Indian Maid Motel, just what they were seeking, luxury class, with a good restaurant and bar.

They were in no hurry. The next morning they decided to stay over another night and explore the town. That afternoon Gretchen said, "I like this place, Jay. Why don't we stay on and see if we can find an apartment that suits us? We don't have to go to Maine, you know. It was just a possibility. Belmont's big enough so that we won't have to mix with people and yet it has the advantages of the lake and sort of a relaxed, small-town atmosphere."

Jay hadn't been keen on her suggestion at first but Gretchen overrode his objections. "We can at least look around, see what we can find. Then, if we don't like it here, we can always leave in a week or two. Besides, it's only the second week of May, too early, really, to go to Maine. It won't be all that warm there yet."

So the decision was made, Gretchen's decision, and for the past two days they had been looking for an apartment. None that they had seen had met their requirements for comfort, space, privacy.

But as they slowed down outside of 519 Lakeview Avenue they agreed that it might suit them. Like its neighbors, the big late-Victorian house was set far back from the street on spacious, well-kept grounds. It was painted gray with black shutters and had a roomy porch across the front. A driveway at one side led back to a building some sixty feet in the rear. Double garage doors with dormer windows above were all that was visible of it from the street. Full-grown trees and shrubbery hid the rest.

"The carriage house," they both said at once. Gretchen added, "The apartment must be upstairs. Very private."

"Best we've seen yet," Jay conceded.

They drove back downtown. It was only a little after four. With time to kill, they had another drink.

Their arrival at the house promptly at five o'clock was greeted by wild barking from a small black and white dog who raced around from in back and pursued them up the front steps.

The woman who answered the door mingled apologies to Jay and Gretchen with admonitions to the animal. "So sorry, I thought he was tied up. But don't worry about him—Billy, be quiet!—he's all bark and no bite ... Billy, if you don't stop this minute I'll shut you in the basement."

"Mrs. Mercer?" Gretchen said.

"Yes. You're Mrs. Addison?"

"And my husband Jay."

"Do come in." Mrs. Mercer held the door wide. "Billy!" Billy subsided, darting around her to get inside.

Only Couples Need Apply 11

She admitted them into a wide front hall wainscoted in oak with a carpeted stairway leading to the second floor.

The hall seemed dim in contrast to outdoors but the room she took them to opening off it was bright with the western sun pouring through the side windows.

"Won't you sit down?"

They settled themselves on an Empire sofa facing their prospective landlady.

She was a tall, big-boned woman with dark eyes and dark hair streaked with gray. She had strong features in a heavy-set face that had never been pretty but still showed traces of a certain handsomeness. Sixtyish, Gretchen thought, with a sturdy athletic look borne out by the golf clubs she had noticed standing in a corner of the hall.

Billy lay down near his mistress, alert gaze fixed on the intruders.

Small talk, the fine May weather, the panoramic view of the lake from the front windows, took up the next few minutes.

Straight ahead of him through an open archway Jay had a different kind of view, the dining room beautifully furnished in period mahogany. Directly opposite was a sideboard with a silver coffee service and antique silver candelabra that were surely collector's items on display.

Wherever his eye fell there were similar pieces, old Chinese vases on the fireplace mantel, a lacquered cabinet in a corner, a portrait over the fireplace that resembled one by Peale in Sherman's house in Paoli, an enameled cigarette box on the table in front of him; in short, a house that showed the accumulation of two or three generations of money well spent.

"How long did you say you expected to stay in Belmont, Mrs. Addison?" Mrs. Mercer inquired presently, assessing her prospective tenants, favorably impressed by their well-groomed appearance.

"Several months at least," Gretchen replied. Like Jay, she had been taking in their surroundings. Mrs. Mercer was obviously not in the usual landlady category.

"Well, let me show you the apartment. We'll go out the back way if you don't mind." The older woman rose and led the way through the house, stopping to pick up her keys—Jay automatically noticed where she kept them—from a brass bowl on the hall table.

They followed her into a spic-and-span kitchen—everything completely modern here, Gretchen observed, except for a pine drop-leaf table and two Windsor chairs under the rear window—out onto a back porch and along a flagstone walk to the driveway.

The carriage house, on closer view, had a third door with a bell and nameplate slot next to one of the rollup doors they had glimpsed from the street. Mrs. Mercer unlocked it, revealing a stairway to the apartment above. Another door at the head of the stairs opened into the living room.

It ran from front to back of the building, pine-paneled, light and cheerful looking with three windows, a dormer in front and one in each of the outside walls. It was comfortably furnished with slip-covered sofa and matching easy chairs, lamps and braided rug, a slant-top desk, a drop-leaf dining table, and chairs on the inside wall between two doors.

These led respectively to a well-equipped kitchen with a utility closet for storage and to a bedroom with a bathroom opening off it. The bedroom had a large clothes closet and there was a linen cupboard in the bathroom.

The whole place looked immaculate, Gretchen noted, and was superior to any furnished apartment she had ever lived in before. They would take it.

"Everything is provided except linens and silver," Mrs. Mercer remarked as the couple went from room to room on their tour of inspection. "There's a TV antenna and telephone jack there by the desk and another telephone jack in the bedroom."

"Very nice," said Gretchen. "Just one thing, though. I don't see where my husband could put his typewriter. Not on the desk, that isn't big enough."

"Typewriter?" Mrs. Mercer, her gaze on Gretchen, missed the startled look that flickered across Jay's face.

"Well, he's planning to write a book," Gretchen explained. "It happens that we've just come into a little money and this summer seems the perfect time for him to get started on it. That's why we're looking for a place like this. Privacy and quiet and yet the lake too. There are lake privileges, aren't there? We both like to swim."

"Oh yes, there's a beach for townspeople ... A book,

Only Couples Need Apply 13

Mr. Addison?" Mrs. Mercer's glance went to Jay. "What will it be about?"

"Oh, no use asking yet," Gretchen interjected hastily. "He keeps it to himself."

"How—interesting, though," Mrs. Mercer said, and then, reverting to the practical, "There must be a table up in the attic that I could have brought over here."

No further mention of the people who were supposed to have looked at the apartment earlier, thought Gretchen. Or of references either. Mrs. Mercer probably used these devices to protect herself against undesirable tenants but in the end relied on her own judgment.

"We'd like to take it," Gretchen made a show of consulting Jay. "Wouldn't we, dear?"

"As long as you're satisfied."

"Well, there is one more point," Mrs. Mercer said. "I ask for two months' rent in advance, one month's regular rent and one that I hold in escrow for thirty days after the apartment is vacated to make sure no damage has been done."

"That seems reasonable enough," Gretchen agreed.

"Good. How soon would you plan to move in?"

"Would day after tomorrow, May 17, be all right? Or would that be too soon?"

"Not at all. My cleaning woman comes tomorrow and I'll have her come out and see that everything's ready for you. Shall we go back to the house now and take care of the details?"

Jay paid her three hundred dollars in cash. "As long as we're going to stay here we'll open a checking account tomorrow at one of the local banks," he said.

Mrs. Mercer made out a receipt and handed over two sets of keys. "Now may I offer you a drink?" she said. "Scotch, Canadian Club, or gin."

"Scotch," they said.

Jay asked if he could help. Mrs. Mercer handed him a beautiful cut-glass decanter.

When he admired it she said, "My greatgrandmother's," and brought out glasses to match.

Crackers and cheese were set out on a Cloisonné plate, the cheese knife taken from a sideboard drawer crammed with silver.

Jay's eyes were everywhere nakedly appraising until

Gretchen found a moment to pinch his arm and whisper, "Stop it."

"But my God," he said when they left, "the stuff that woman has lying around must be worth thousands. Just in the china cabinet, for instance. Did you get a look at it? And that diamond ring she was wearing, three or four carats, knock your eye out. Not to mention her pearls. Real ones, not cultured, worth plenty, let me tell you."

He slowed down for a stop light turning red. Gretchen gave him a level look.

"Forget it, Jay," she said. "We agreed to take the summer off, didn't we?"

There was a note of disdain, impatience, irritation in her voice. It was often there for Jay, her partner, her lover, her tool.

As she was his.

2

They were up early the next morning, out of their motel, with a busy day ahead of them, by nine o'clock. They went first to the Belmont Trust Company and opened a joint checking account, using their new address, 519½ Lakeview Avenue, and depositing, with a new car in mind, ten thousand dollars in traveler's checks. Their next stop was at a savings bank down the street where they opened a joint savings account with five thousand in traveler's checks. This, with cash on hand, should be enough money to live on for the summer, Gretchen said. They would transfer it from savings to their checking account as they needed it, meanwhile letting it draw interest.

They drove back to I-84 and took it to downtown Hartford.

Apartments for rent in the Hartford *Courant* supplied them with a fictitious address. They used it at two different banks, opening joint savings accounts as John and

Only Couples Need Apply

Greta Loomis with deposits of fifteen thousand in traveler's checks.

They had twenty-five thousand more under still another name but Gretchen said that could wait. "A New Haven bank just to be on the safe side," she said. "We'll make that another trip the end of the week."

Each carried a thousand dollars emergency money at all times. Jay kept his, ten one-hundred-dollar bills, in the secret compartment of his wallet, dismissing as a nuisance the money belt Gretchen suggested he should buy. She more careful with hers, kept it in cloth bags pinned to her underwear.

When they finished their business at the second bank they checked the classified section of the telephone directory and set out to buy a secondhand portable typewriter, Jay still protesting that it wasn't necessary, that not all writers used them. "It's crazy," he said. "I can't even type."

"It looks more convincing," Gretchen said. "You don't have to turn out much manuscript just starting your first book, but there should be a typewriter. And if I have to, I'll do some of the typing for you."

They bought a portable in fairly good condition for thirty-five dollars. Then, after a late lunch, they went to a department store where Gretchen produced a list of what they had to buy, bed linens, place mats, towels, a set of inexpensive stainless steel flatware and other incidentals they would need to set up housekeeping.

"Now there's just the book," she said when they had taken their purchases to their car in a nearby parking lot.

"Book?"

"Oh Jay, do try to keep your wits about you," Gretchen exclaimed. "You agreed last night that we'd hunt around in some secondhand bookstore—"

"Oh yes. Some novel no one ever heard of by some author no one ever heard of published fifty years or more ago so that it's safe to crib the plot for the book I'm supposed to be writing." His voice took on an impatient note. "It all sounds very elaborate to me but at least you did say you'd be the one to read it and make up an outline I can use if I ever should have to talk to anyone about it."

"I will."

They found a secondhand bookstore. Gretchen did the

browsing and searching while Jay concentrated on a rack of new paperbacks picking out several that he hadn't read.

Eventually Gretchen rejoined him at a counter where he had propped himself up to wait for her. "This will do, I think." She handed him a novel, *The Man Who Didn't Make Good*, published in 1913.

"Never heard of the author or the book," she said. "Look what good condition it's in nearly sixty years later. No wonder, the dreary plot it has. Boy with hangup on his domineering grandmother and all that—the kind of thing that's being written again nowadays."

"As long as I don't have to read it myself," Jay said flipping the pages disinterestedly.

Gretchen paid a quarter for the book and tucked it into her shopping bag.

"Now a dictionary," she said, and bought a desk standard Webster that showed suitable signs of usage.

On their way out she stopped short. "Oh, paper." She turned back to ask where it could be bought.

"Charter Oak Stationery Shop, three doors up the street," she was told.

They bought a ream of yellow paper.

Walking back to the car Gretchen felt pleased with herself. "We're really organized now except for groceries. Let's stop at the apartment on our way back to the motel and drop off the things we've bought. We might as well make up the bed, too, while we're there. We'll have enough to do tomorrow, moving in and all."

"This will be the longest time we've every played house," Jay said. He gave her arm a quick squeeze. "Who knows, one day when we've got plenty of money we might make it permanent."

"We might," she agreed and gave him the slow provocative smile that always stirred him. "We just might."

Mrs. Mercer's Buick was gone from her half of the garage when they arrived at the apartment.

They carried their purchases upstairs, unwrapped and put them away and made up the bed.

A solid-looking table had been added since yesterday. But when Jay said he would bring up the typewriter Gretchen shook her head. "It should be brought with our luggage tomorrow. You wouldn't take it along on a shopping trip."

Only Couples Need Apply 17

"You actually expect Mrs. Mercer snooping around up here tonight?"

"I don't know if she will or not. Sometime soon, though, she will. That's why we're going to have to have manuscript on display."

"Chrissake, this is nuts," said Jay. "Let's go get a drink. We've had a hell of a long day."

They checked out of their motel the next morning. By noon they were unpacked and settled in the apartment although not without a brief dispute over Gretchen's wigs, Jay frowning as he carried the cases upstairs.

"Damn it all, how many times do I have to ask you to get rid of them?" he said.

"And how many times have I told you I won't?" Gretchen retorted. "Makes no sense when they cost over three hundred apiece. Anyway, what other colors could I get next time? Flaming red, maybe, so that everyone would notice me? More to the point is your gun. How about getting rid of that?"

Jay did not answer. The gun was his business. He had told Gretchen over and over that he'd never had one he liked better; and that there was plenty of time to get rid of it after he had bought another that suited him as well.

A shopping center not too far away was next on their agenda. It provided a liquor store, drugstore, a branch of the Belmont Trust Company, a hardware store, laundromat, various other shops, a restaurant where they had lunch, and a large supermarket.

"But we won't use this one all the time," Gretchen said as they went up and down the aisles filling their cart from her list. "Or the laundromat. Or any of the other stores here either. Just as well not to let our faces get too familiar anywhere."

"You think of everything," Jay remarked. "You're like the guy in Julius Caesar. You think too much."

"Do I?" Gretchen eyed him coldly. "Maybe that's why we've stayed out of trouble so far. You don't do enough thinking yourself. Or look far enough ahead."

"Why should I?" His glance was as cold as hers. "You're only too ready to do it for both of us. You're good at it, I'll admit that."

"Well then, why make it sound like a fault if you're

willing to concede it's a virtue?" Gretchen's tone was only slightly mollified.

Mrs. Mercer's car was still in the garage as it had been earlier when they got back to the apartment. Gretchen went over to see her after they had put the groceries away. She started to go to the back door, changed course and went around to the front door instead. More of her looking ahead, she reflected. Since they planned to keep their distance all summer, they should put themselves on a formal footing with their landlady from the beginning and try to maintain it.

The front door stood open to the late afternoon sunshine. Billy lay on the mat outside and leaped up, barking and wagging his tail at the same time, as she climbed the steps. "Oh, shut up," she said.

A cleaning woman answered the door. Gretchen introduced herself as the new tenant.

"Oh yes, I was out back getting things ready for you yesterday," the woman said. "But Mrs. Mercer ain't here. She's out playing bridge."

"I saw her car in the garage . . ."

"One of the other ladies picked her up."

"Well, I wonder if I could use her phone? It's just to call the phone company and arrange to have one installed in the apartment."

The woman let her in and waited near the door while Gretchen used the phone in the kitchen. As she was leaving the woman said, "It just came to me, Mrs.—uh—?"

"Addison."

"That if you're looking for someone to do your cleaning—only half a day, I guess—my sister-in-law might oblige you. I couldn't take on another job myself—only came here an extra day this week as a favor to Mrs. Mercer—"

"Thank you, but I don't believe we'll need anyone," Gretchen replied. "I'm sure I'll be able to take care of the apartment myself. Besides, my husband will be writing a book and wouldn't want to have anyone coming in to disturb his routine."

"A book?" The woman looked impressed. "Imagine that. How long will it take?"

"A year, at least."

"My, I'd never have the patience."

Only Couples Need Apply 19

This qualification for writing a book amused Gretchen.

She felt satisfied as well as amused when she left. The cleaning woman worked in other houses and would spread the word that Jay was writing a book and wanted no interruptions. It would tend to discourage callers.

Mrs. Mercer received the same impression when she got home from her bridge game and went over to ask if they had everything they needed.

The typewriter was already on the table, a stack of yellow paper and the dictionary lined up beside it.

"Well, you look all set, Mr. Addison," she commented. "I hope the table will do."

"It's just fine, thanks. I'm going to try to get to work tomorrow."

"It's an ideal place for it," Gretchen said. "So nice and quiet, Jay should accomplish wonders. Being in a strange town, not knowing people or going out a lot will help too. Jay was saying just before you came, Mrs. Mercer, that he hopes I won't mind if we just keep to ourselves this summer so there'll be nothing to disturb him."

"Well, there's plenty going on in Belmont, especially in the summer, but no need for you to take part in it if you'd prefer not to," Mrs. Mercer replied.

She left a few minutes later pleased with her new tenants. Such an attractive young couple and making it plain that they meant to live very quietly, no parties or people back and forth while Mr. Addison wrote his book.

Ideal tenants she informed a friend who called right after she got home. From what they'd said, it seemed as if she would hardly know they were there. How old were they? Well, she wasn't sure.

She conjured up an image of Gretchen's smooth untroubled face. "Mrs. Addison must be in her early twenties," she said. "He's probably a little older. I doubt they've been married very long, not even having their own furniture yet."

Of course she would keep an eye on things for a while, she added, new tenants and all. But she anticipated no problems.

Gretchen had bought a steak and a bottle of wine to celebrate their moving in. Jay washed the dishes.

That was the way it had been in other furnished apartments they'd had. Gretchen, a good cook, got their meals, Jay did most of the cleaning up afterward.

They had nightcaps before they went to bed.

"We'll rent a color TV tomorrow," Jay said.

"Tomorrow afternoon," Gretchen said. "In the morning I'm going to start outlining *The Man Who Didn't Make Good* for you."

"Oh hell," he said resignedly.

"The perfect cover," she said firmly.

He dropped the subject. A little later he asked, "What was the name of that guy—you know, the one in Philadelphia? Funny, I know it as well as I know my own name but when I tried to think of it just now I couldn't."

"Sherman. William Sherman."

"Oh yes. Damnedest thing, isn't it, the way you can forget names?"

Gretchen had not forgotten it ...

3

He was her first employer, senior partner in the law firm of Bryce, Sherman, Hunt and Gannon, a sixty-year-old widower when Gretchen, just out of junior college with an associate degree in secretarial science, went to work for the firm, one of three young women in the stenographic pool.

Within a year her competence caught Sherman's attention. He began asking specifically for her from time to time as a substitute for his ailing elderly secretary. Within another year the secretary died—the first time death served to Gretchen's advantage—and she was promoted to take her place.

No reason she shouldn't have been, bright, efficient, reliable as she was, cosseting Sherman in many unobtrusive ways, handling various matters herself that her predecessor would have dumped in his lap. Before long she made herself indispensable to him. So much so, that when he suffered a stroke in December of her fourth year, as his private secretary, she was able to take care of all sorts of unfinished business, legal and personal, on his behalf.

By February he was better, allowed to work a little at home, getting around in a wheelchair from first-floor bedroom to study and back. Gretchen, who had an apartment she had furnished herself in Lansdowne, began driving out to his old stone house in Paoli two or three times a week to work with him there.

He put her in charge of all his financial affairs. She paid his taxes, household bills including weekly checks for his housekeeper and part-time yardman, coped with a plumber, kept in touch with his broker.

William Sherman was a man of considerable means who invested his money in various ways. The final mark of his trust in her came in April. He signed the authorization that gave her access to his safe deposit box, telling her he wanted a complete list brought up to date of stocks and bonds, real estate deeds, insurance policies, everything now in the box, including his late wife's jewelry.

He was showing steady improvement by that time. His speech was still slurred, he had little use of his left arm or leg but if there were no setbacks during the summer he might, by fall, his doctor said, be able to get back to his office for a day or two a week.

Meanwhile, he relied more and more on Gretchen. He took to calling her his Girl Friday when she began to stay on to give him dinner on his housekeeper's Wednesday afternoons off. He didn't know what he would do without her, he said.

She met Jay Hubbard at a cocktail party not long after Sherman's stroke. There was no one else important in either of their lives just then, no hindrance to their spending, within a week or two, most of their free time together.

Jay, a native Philadelphian, lived nearby, sharing an apartment with a friend from college days. He had left college himself during the second semester of his sophomore year. With no training in any field, just his good looks and personable manner to recommend him, the best he could do after Army service was a salesman's job in a jewelry store in Philadelphia where, he told Gretchen, he made a reasonably decent living but that was all.

"Nothing like what I'd probably be making if I'd been able to finish college," he said. "My mother's fault"—a resentful note came into his voice—"electing to die when she did. Very sly and bitchy of her, that's what it was, not telling me she had put my father's whole estate into an annuity. So that when she died and expenses were paid out of her insurance, there I was with only about eight hundred dollars between me and welfare."

"But couldn't you have got some sort of student loan to finish?" Gretchen asked.

Jay shrugged. "I wasn't that good a student. Didn't even know what I wanted to major in—Penn State offered no courses in how to live well without working—and there was the draft waiting for me. So I served my time and then the guy I had roomed with got his father to give me a job in his jewelry store." Another shrug. "That was it, I took the path of least resistance."

As he always would, Gretchen thought, having no illusions about him from the start.

They began sleeping together not long after they met. The pleasure they shared in bed deepened their need of each other as the weeks and months passed. By May, after a number of conversations on how much more they wanted from life than their future prospects offered, Gretchen found herself ready to bring into the open possibilities she had been mulling over for using William Sherman as a gateway to a better life.

She brought the subject up one night when they had gone out to dinner and then back to her apartment. After lovemaking and an interval for cigarettes she said, "Make us a drink, Jay. There's something I want to talk to you about."

All her life, as far back as she could remember, had been leading to this moment ...

Only child, five years old, sitting at table, father wrapped in one of his icy silences, mother fluttering over them. "More potatoes, Harry? ... Drink your milk, Gretchen, or you can't have any dessert."

Caught in the middle of this, bewildered, frightened, Gretchen became convinced that she must be to blame for

Only Couples Need Apply

her father's silences, sometimes lasting for days, her mother's inane flutterings.

Years later, looking back, she realized that his silences were actually directed at her mother, his weapon for punishing her every offense.

He was easily offended, a bright but touchy man unable to get ahead in life; a man who worked at a machine in a Merlin factory, sour with jealousy of fellow workers not nearly so bright as he was himself and yet somehow promoted to better jobs than he would ever have; a man who never laughed or even smiled much at the best of times; who paid little attention to his daughter—except to find fault—and never took her anywhere.

Rage that would never leave her supplanted guilt when Gretchen was eight or nine, beginning to realize that she was a have-not living on the fringe of the haves in a shabby little house on what was a country road in her grandfather's day but now an affluent suburb of Merlin. The children she went to school with lived in fine new houses taking for granted luxuries far beyond her reach. She had none at all.

"No, Gretchen, you can't have that . . . No, Gretchen, it costs too much."

Like the bride doll. "No, Gretchen, we just couldn't afford one like Lucia's. Put it right out of your head."

Instead, Gretchen stole the doll the next day. Once she had it safely hidden, though, she discovered that her chief pleasure in it came from the stealing itself and having got away with it . . .

Her father was a failure then. A tyrant inside their four walls, a failure everywhere else. Her mother was a fool, constantly fluttering, trying to please him. Contempt for both kept pace with the rage Gretchen carried around inside her.

"If I said I didn't want anything else at all for Christmas, could I have an English bike like Susan Hume's?"

"You should know better than to ask, Gretchen. We couldn't possibly afford it."

She was eleven that Christmas. A year later, going into junior high, it wouldn't have mattered. But that Christmas it mattered more than anything else in the world.

She yearned over Susan's bike. Susan, acting superior,

wouldn't even let her ride it. But Gretchen paid her back. She waited until a Sunday when the Humes were away, took the bike from their garage, rode it down to the river and threw it in.

Before she was twelve Gretchen decided that if her parents wouldn't get things for her she would get them for herself. She began to shoplift. Clear gray eyes, candid look combined with facile lies saved her more than once from being caught. Later, she relied on experience. At home, a new dress worn under her own walking out of the store became a thrift shop bargain. Smaller articles were smuggled in and out, sometimes sold for spending money.

The year she was sixteen brought awareness that social lines were beginning to be clearly drawn in high school and that she was being left out of some of the more exclusive parties. Jamie Ballard's pool party, marking the end of their junior year, would be the most exclusive one of all. Gretchen was not invited. Jamie had always been immune to the beauty that drew so many of the other boys to her and alienated so many of the girls.

Gretchen's revenge went beyond her expectation. In the pell-mell crush at the end of the school day chance put Jamie just ahead of her at the top of the stairs. A hard push with both hands sent him hurtling down the full flight knocking down others in the way. No one else was seriously injured but Jamie was taken to the hospital with a broken leg. He could only say someone had pushed him. He couldn't say who it was. Gretchen had slipped back into the crowd.

The pool party was canceled.

Although fees were minimal at Merlin Community College, Gretchen had to pay them herself, take care of all her expenses by working part-time.

"We can't help you," her parents said. "We can't afford it."

Gretchen no longer answered this familiar plaint. It wasn't worth it. She hated them in silence, her whole being concentrated on escaping from them and the poky little city of Merlin into a larger world.

An associate degree in secretarial science was the key that would open the door to it.

Her first year she worked in the college library. Her

Only Couples Need Apply

second year, through a contact she made there, she got a better-paying job, receptionist in a doctor's office three weekday evenings and Saturday afternoons.

The doctor was a family man in his early fifties, the father of three children. While he was still in medical school he had married a girl with money and social position. The money and position remained; the girl had become a fat jealous wife ready to make a scene if he even looked at another woman at a party.

But in his office he ruled supreme. He hired Gretchen. Within a month she had taken his measure. Within two, lingering after the last patient of the evening had left, she began going out for a drink with him at discreet, out-of-town places. Within three, they were registering at equally discreet motels.

He fell head over heels in love with her as only an older man, driven by the feeling that he has missed the best in life, could; aware all the while of the difference in their ages and that a girl as young and lovely as Gretchen couldn't possibly love him back, a middle-aged balding man, cheating on his wife.

He tried to blind himself to this reality, lavishing gifts and attentions on her, making the most of what she gave—or rather, let him take from her—using as well as being used.

Gretchen kept a detailed record of their affair, dates and times when they were together, where they went, what they did, things he told her about himself.

The week she was graduated from Merlin Community College she went to a motel with him for the last time and enunciated her demands. Ten thousand dollars, she said, enough to buy her a car, give her a start on a new life. A week, she said, to come up with the money in cash. Otherwise, she would go to his wife, wreck his marriage, create a scandal he could never live down.

Crushed, stunned, his fantasy world in ruins around him, he had no choice but to agree.

A few days after she got the money Gretchen left Merlin, promising herself as she boarded the bus to Philadelphia and waved a last good-by to her parents that she would never come back.

She wrote them two letters the first year she was gone, the next year one. After that, only Christmas cards. Until the Sherman project; that ended her last tenuous link with them.

4

"Treasury Bonds, Jay," Gretchen said when he had made their drinks. "Payable to bearer. Sherman has forty thousand dollars' worth of them in his safe deposit box. We could also convert into cash Mrs. Sherman's jewelry. I've checked it. Three or four diamond rings, earrings, a diamond wristwatch. And a big square-cut emerald ring. Aren't emeralds sometimes more valuable than diamonds, darling?"

"They can be. Depends. The Treasury Bonds—don't they have serial numbers or something?"

"Yes, but if we sold them right away . . ."

Jay, stretched out on the bed beside her, lit a cigarette and blew smoke rings at the ceiling. "How come you haven't taken them on your own? The old boy's sent you to his box three or four times."

"Just been thinking and thinking about it. Now, though, the time's come to act. And here you are, working in a jewelry store. You could remove stones from their settings, couldn't you?"

"Don't see why not."

"And the stones become unidentifiable out of their settings, don't they?"

"Unless they're something real special, yes."

"These aren't. But would sell for quite a lot, I'm sure."

Jay turned his head to look at her. "What have you got in mind, Gretchen? The bonds, for instance. Would we even have a chance to cash them before the old boy squawked?"

"The way I've been working it out, yes. Today is Satur-

Only Couples Need Apply

day. A week from next Friday his housekeeper will be going away overnight to attend her son's wedding in North Carolina. She leaves early that morning and doesn't get back until late Saturday. Meanwhile, I'm to stay over and look after Mr. Sherman. Which gives us plenty of leeway."

"And how do you get him to hand over the key to his safe deposit box?"

Gretchen sat up in bed her hair falling forward over her bare shoulders. "You handle that end, sweetie," she said softly. "You point a gun at him while he gives me the key and also makes out a check; payable to cash, for most of what he has in his checking account. It's usually between three and four thousand. You keep the gun on him while I drive in to Philadelphia, cash the check at his bank, get the bonds and jewelry out of his safe deposit box and then get the bonds cashed at another bank—or banks, maybe, asking for the money in cash."

"Sweet Jesus, I don't even own a gun!"

She gave him a slow smile, trailed her fingers up and down his arm. "Not all that hard to get, are they?"

"But, my God, we'd be on the run . . ."

"Not necessarily. And we'd have forty-odd thousand in cash, plus the jewelry we could sell later, plus the experience we gained. I'm looking ahead, you see."

"What about Sherman? Would you leave him tied up or something?"

"Or something."

"Meaning what?"

She tossed her head. "Let that go for the moment, darling. May I have a cigarette, please?"

Jay lit one for her and said, "Seems to me you're doing it the hard way. Why not just wait until the next time he sends you on some errand to his box?"

"No, now's the time, the housekeeper going away and all. Besides which, there's his granddaughter's wedding in the offing next month."

"Oh . . ."

"I told you. Daughter of his only son who died several years ago. The widow remarried and lives in Binghamton, New York. Sherman's giving his granddaughter all his wife's jewelry for a wedding present. That enters into it because he's doing so well lately. For all I know, he might want me to take him into town by that time and go to his bank himself."

"Even so—"

"I've thought it all out. Better than fifty thousand. We could do a lot with it, darling."

"If the cops didn't catch us first."

"Me, not necessarily you. I'd be a major suspect if anything went wrong but you wouldn't really be involved at all. You could disguise yourself, wear gloves so that you wouldn't leave fingerprints. Whereas mine would be all over the place. After months of going there, I couldn't hope to get rid of all of them. Another time I'd be more careful."

He gave her a startled look. "You thinking of a life of crime?"

Gretchen leaned over and kissed him on the cheek. "Possibly, darling. But just until we get a real nestegg together."

She would reveal no more of her plan that night. Let him absorb, get used to that much of it tonight, she said, and they would talk about the rest tomorrow.

By the next day Jay was ready for the rest, the bare bones of it that would insure their own safety.

Gretchen had it worked out. She would call Jay from Philadelphia as soon as she had cashed Sherman's check and the bonds. The moment he hung up the phone he was to kill Sherman.

She watched Jay closely as she said this. His role was the crux of the matter, the great divide in their relationship.

Jay took a deep breath, blinked once or twice, looked away, looked back. "Okay," he said.

Gretchen waited a moment, went on to what would be her story for the police. She would tell them that Sherman had received a phone call that morning, had then sent her to the bank in Philadelphia to cash a check and take out of his safe deposit box a sealed unmarked manila envelope and all his wife's jewelry. When she got back to the house, she would say, there was a car in the driveway—no, she hadn't noticed it particularly—and a man she'd never met before, a Mr. Beale, with Mr. Sherman in his study. She had given Sherman the money, envelope, and jewelry. He had then sent her back to his office in Philadelphia to do

Only Couples Need Apply

some work there. It was late afternoon when she returned. She found Sherman shot to death, the man Beale gone and also the money, the envelope, and the jewelry.

During the next few days Gretchen and Jay went over and over her plan for this, their first project, smoothing, perfecting it. Then Jay bought a gun.

The following week the housekeeper left at seven Friday morning with her daughter and son-in-law who came to pick her up. Gretchen arrived just as they were leaving, prepared breakfast for Sherman and herself and got him settled in his study with the morning paper. The old stone house, basking in the early June sunlight, seemed to take on the somnolence of its semirural surroundings. There wasn't even the yardman to disturb the quiet. He didn't come Fridays.

There was only Jay ringing the doorbell at eight-thirty, his car already safely out of sight in the vacant half of the double garage.

Gretchen admitted him, waited while he donned a stocking mask and took him into Sherman's study, a terrifying, faceless figure, so shocking to Sherman that he couldn't really believe at first what was happening. But with Jay pointing a gun at him and Gretchen telling him what he had to do, he made out a check for thirty-five hundred dollars and handed over the key to his safe deposit box.

Gretchen left at once for Philadelphia. She cashed the check first at Sherman's bank and took the bonds and jewelry out of safe deposit. Then, wearing dark glasses and a scarf to hide her hair, she cashed the eight five-thousand-dollar bonds at different banks.

It was midafternoon before she was ready to call Jay to tell him that everything was under control before she went to Sherman's office to establish her alibi.

"Okay to go ahead with it," she said.

"Not necessary," he said. "Taken care of by natural causes. Another stroke or something?"

"What?"

"You heard me. No need to bother with alibis now. Just get back here fast as you can."

The good luck of it! The incredible good luck. Too good to be true, Gretchen thought, driving back to the house, hurrying into the study. But there was William

Sherman, body sagged over the arm of his wheelchair, eyes glazed in death.

"When did it happen?"

"About an hour before you called. Jesus, I was just sitting here and then, all of a sudden—"

Gretchen took instant charge. She handed over the money and jewelry to Jay. "Go straight home," she said. "Wait to hear from me. Pete's gone for the weekend, isn't he?"

"Yes, I'll have the place to myself."

"All right, go home and stay there. You've had a stomach upset just like you said when you called your boss this morning and you've been in bed all day."

Jay left. Gretchen went to the file and destroyed the list of the contents of Sherman's safe deposit box before she called his doctor. Her mind worked with the speed of a computer revising her story while she waited for him.

As soon as the doctor heard the new version of it he called the police. Gretchen then told it all over again for their benefit.

According to the new version, a man who gave his name as Beale had arrived at the house a little before nine that morning and asked to see Mr. Sherman.

What did the man look like? Well, that was sort of hard to say. Nothing out of the ordinary about him. Just a middle-aged man, maybe past fifty, gray hair, brown eyes, about average height, dressed in light blue—or was it green?—slacks and sport shirt.

Mr. Sherman said he would see him and she took him to the study, went back herself to her improvised office in the sitting room. A few minutes later Mr. Sherman pressed the buzzer connected to her desk, told her to show Mr. Beale out and that he would then have some things he wanted her to do.

She took Mr. Beale to the door—no, she hadn't noticed what kind of a car he was driving, just that it was some dark color—and returned to Mr. Sherman.

He sent her to his bank in Philadelphia with a check for thirty-five hundred dollars, made out to cash. He also gave her the key to his safe deposit box and said she was to bring back from it a sealed, unmarked manila envelope and all his wife's jewelry.

She had thought the whole thing a bit peculiar—he had

Only Couples Need Apply

never, for instance, drawn out that much money in cash before—but it wasn't her business to question him, only to do as she was told.

She returned around noon, she continued, gave him the money, envelope, and boxes of jewelry and suggested lunch. He didn't want any, he said. This had bothered her but there wasn't much she could do about it.

Around one o'clock—Gretchen had worked out the timing carefully—Mr. Beale had returned. She had taken him to the study and gone back to her desk.

He had stayed only a few minutes and let himself out. She heard the front door open and close, the car drive away. She waited a little while and then went to the study and reminded Mr. Sherman that he'd had no lunch. He said again that he didn't want any. He seemed upset, just sitting there looking out the window.

She withdrew. He asked her to close the door as she left. If there'd been any sound, any outcry from Mr. Sherman after that she hadn't heard it. Of course that might be because the room where she worked was on the other side of the house. Finally, though, she got so uneasy that she went back to the study and found Mr. Sherman dead in his chair. What time was that? Oh, she wasn't watching the time but it was shortly before she called the doctor.

She had no chance to call Jay until nine o'clock that night. The next day she saw him briefly, just long enough to tell him everything was going along fine.

She was questioned again that day by the police. The trend of their questions indicated that they were thinking of blackmail in their search for the nonexistent Beale. Gretchen enlarged on her story by adding that Mr. Sherman had seemed surprised—perhaps shocked was a better word—to have him turn up yesterday morning.

An autopsy revealed that Sherman had died of a coronary thrombosis. No suspicion attached to Gretchen. Her job status, the dead man's complete trust in her saw to that.

"The marvelous luck of it," she rejoiced to Jay. "All we have to do now is wait it out for a bit."

Jay handed in a month's notice at the jewelry store. Gretchen went through the motions of going back to the law firm but said she thought a change of scene was what she really needed. She was given three months' severance pay and excellent references she would never use.

"California," she said. "Lots of old people out there with money. I've got some ideas about them."

They sold their two cars and headed west in a rental car, stopping off here and there to sell the late Mrs. Sherman's jewelry. It brought them something over four thousand dollars, not half its real value, Jay said.

Gretchen didn't like that. But still, considering the good luck of Sherman's death from natural causes, she had no real complaints as they traveled at a leisurely rate across the country, staying at the best places, eating in the best restaurants, wearing the best clothes.

Eventually they reached California.

5

The day after they moved into Mrs. Mercer's apartment they bought a new car and wrote a check to pay the full cost of it. Later that day they applied for Connecticut driver's licenses.

When their new car was delivered the following Monday they turned in the rental car they had been using. The next day they drove to New Haven.

They cashed the rest of their traveler's checks in New Haven banks. As John and Glenda Dunn, they put fifteen thousand of the money they received into a joint savings account. The remaining twelve thousand, they decided, should be treated as a cash reserve fund and be kept in a safe deposit box with the unsold jewelry.

Gretchen suggested that they look over motels while they were in New Haven. "Just in case some emergency comes up this summer and we have to separate," she said. "Just to play it safe."

They settled on the West Rock Motel as a meeting

Only Couples Need Apply 33

place and Mr. and Mrs. John Collins as the name they would use if they ever had to register there.

They did a little shopping after that and stopped off for dinner at a restaurant near New Haven on the way home.

"We've had a good day," Jay said, reaching out an arm to draw her close to him when they were back in the car.

"Plenty of them ahead," Gretchen replied confidently, resting her head on his shoulder.

"Except that we still need a lot more money," he said.

"We'll get it. We just have to take it easy for now, take our time."

With money and jewelry safely in banks, bankbooks locked up in their strongbox, they were ready to settle into a summer routine.

Gretchen finished reading *The Man Who Didn't Make Good* and typed a synopsis of it for Jay.

Then the problem arose that he couldn't—or wouldn't, she thought irritatedly—start producing some semblance of a book.

"But you have to," she protested the second morning that the same blank sheet of paper remained in the typewriter. "It's our reason for being here, for needing the privacy we've talked about to Mrs. Mercer. You know very well she'll come snooping one of these days and there's got to be finished manuscript for her benefit."

"Can't help that," Jay said, giving her a lazy uncontrite smile from the sofa where he lay sprawled out. "Can't write, never could. Never got better than a C in English composition in my life."

"But Jay—"

"You do it. Your idea, sprung on me without warning, from the beginning. You should have said you were the writer."

"You know that wouldn't have looked right. It would have drawn attention to us, people wondering why you didn't have a job. Gigolo, they'd have said."

"Well then, you can still do the writing without anyone knowing about it. First, though"—he reached up as she stood over him and pulled her down onto the sofa—"I've got better ideas than fiddling around with a dreary old book." His mouth came down on hers, his arms closed tight around her.

So it was Gretchen who had to work on the book, cutting, updating, altering.

"Two or three pages a day are enough," she said. "After all, you're supposed to be a beginning writer and not get much done at first."

"Cross things out, change them a lot, too, don't I?" he inquired.

"Suppose so. Meanwhile," she seated herself at the typewriter trying to keep her voice light, the undertone of irritation out of it as she added, "there'll have to be a different division of work around here. You make the bed, tidy things up."

Pages of manuscript began to grow. The week after Memorial Day, when they decided to spend a few days at Cape Cod before school closed and it got too crowded, there were well over twenty pages completed.

"Respectable showing," Gretchen said, making a neat stack of it and closing the typewriter. "Enough to impress Mrs. Mercer."

"What makes you so sure she'll come nosing around while we're gone? She's not the usual run of landladies."

"We're not the usual run of tenants, either," Gretchen pointed out. "Coming here out of nowhere, keeping to ourselves, no visible means of support—I'd wonder about us if I were in her shoes. Leaving around this dull manuscript that no one would want to read, should put a stop to it, put you once and for all in a compartment labeled writer. They're supposed to be different from other people and live different lives. At least from things I've read."

"I wouldn't know," said Jay without interest.

"Well, I'll go over now before we leave and let her know the coast will be clear for the next two or three days. You might as well get our suitcases down to the car while I'm gone."

Billy, sunning himself out back on Mrs. Mercer's terrace, leaped up when Gretchen came out of the apartment. He went through his usual performance of barking and wagging his tail simultaneously but his heart wasn't in it; he had Jay and Gretchen's rights and boundaries established, by this time, in his mind. However, he still felt it necessary to keep an eye out and trotted along beside

Gretchen as she followed her procedure of going around to the front door.

She was wearing a turquoise blue pants suit. Her earrings, turquoise in an antique gold setting, matched it. Their design made them too distinctive to sell and they weren't all that valuable anyway, she had told Jay, picking them out of Mrs. Russell's jewelry. But only since they had come to Connecticut had she felt it was really safe to start wearing them.

Mrs. Mercer answered the door. "Oh, good morning, Mrs. Addison," she said. "What an attractive outfit. And the earrings just match. They're so pretty; unusual-looking too."

"Thank you. They were my great-aunt's."

"Won't you come in? Down, Billy." She gave the dog a reproving tap on the nose as he leaped up for attention.

"I'm afraid I don't have time. Jay and I are just leaving for the Cape. He's been working on his book quite hard but finds it slow going at the start. I told him it might help to get away from it for two or three days."

"That's a good idea," Mrs. Mercer said. "Beautiful weather, too. I'm sure you'll enjoy it."

"Well," Gretchen turned toward the steps. "I just wanted you to know so that you wouldn't wonder what had become of us."

"I'm glad you did. I hope you'll tell me whenever you're going to be away overnight, Mrs. Addison. Then I'll try to keep an eye on your place."

No doubt she would, Gretchen thought as she said good-by.

Back in the apartment she went from room to room, leaving the closet door in the bedroom slightly ajar, manuscript pages not quite evenly stacked on the typewriter table, a hair placed so that it would dislodge if the desk top was opened.

Jay lounged in the doorway bored by these stratagems.

"You better pray the old girl comes snooping while we're gone," he said as they went down to their car. "It's the only way you can justify all this business of typewriter and manuscript and me writing a book. Me, of all people!"

"But don't you see—" Gretchen broke off. She had learned long ago that there many things Jay never would see. Or, even more importantly, foresee. She had to do that for both of them.

Billy was still outside when they drove off and rushed to the edge of the driveway in a frenzy of barking.

"Damn pest," said Jay.

Mrs. Mercer saw them leave, struck once again by the thought of what a handsome young couple they made, so close, so devoted to each other too; and as tenants no trouble at all, the nicest she'd had the four years she had been renting the apartment.

She sighed as their car vanished from sight. Her own youth was long gone—she would never again be setting off on a vacation trip with a husband who loved her.

It gave her a lonely feeling. She would go out and do some gardening. A perfect day for it and the best way she could think of to shake off the blues that had settled on her so suddenly.

Mrs. Mercer resisted the temptation to take a look around the apartment until early evening. She had not been inside it since the night her tenants arrived and she had gone over to see if they were comfortably settled. But in their absence, with the setting sun reflected in fiery rays off the front windows, she was able to persuade herself that she had better check to see if lights had been left on.

She didn't give herself time to weigh the matter but went at once to get her keys from the hall table. A minute or so later she was across the yard climbing the stairs to the apartment.

The sunset dazzled her at first when she entered the living room. She moved out of its range and stood looking about her, noting with approval how clean and orderly the room was. Gretchen Addison wasn't at all like some of the careless young wives who had been her predecessors.

Mrs. Mercer's tentative steps took her next into the bedroom. Bed neatly made, bureau top free of clutter, no clothes strewn around. There was just the closet door standing slightly ajar. Instinctively, she was so neat herself, she walked over and closed it.

She went on to the kitchen. No messy cupboards or counter tops, no dishes left in the sink. She glanced into the utility closet. Cleaning equipment, several pieces of luggage including two hatboxes—that was what she

Only Couples Need Apply 37

thought Gretchen's wig cases were—nothing else much. The Addisons, she reflected, didn't have many possessions of their own.

Mrs. Mercer returned to the living room. The Governor Winthrop desk caught her eye. Without meaning to, she found herself opening it for a quick look inside, instantly closing it, feeling ashamed of herself. Not that there was much to see. Nearly all the compartments were empty.

Whatever mail the Addisons received—they were renting a box at the post office, they had said—wasn't kept in the desk. Or perhaps not kept at all. Some people kept it, some didn't.

It occurred to her that they probably received very little mail. That somehow they seemed—was the word isolated?—from the rest of the world as if they had come into it suddenly here in Belmont with just their personal belongings, not even the few household effects they had acquired since.

But wasn't it always more or less that way with a new young couple coming into town, renting her furnished apartment?

No, not really. The Claytons, for instance, her last tenants, had arrived loaded down with wedding presents and had turned out to be something of a nuisance with relatives appearing weekends and friends they made in Belmont coming and going.

It was bound to be different, of course, with the Addisons. They had said they wanted privacy for him to start a book.

Her eyes strayed to the work table she had provided. There was Mr. Addison's typewriter which certainly looked as if it had had lots of use, on one side of it a stack of fresh paper and on the other—she crossed the room for a closer look—pages already written.

These lay face down to the right of the typewriter, twenty-two in all at the beginning of chapter three.

Her glance skimmed the first page. The story opened with a lonely little boy dominated by an aunt—no, grandmother it turned out to be on page two. An orphan then? It seemed so on page three.

She skimmed a few more pages and put them down, straightening the edges. Not very interesting, she thought. Autobiographical, probably. Didn't most young writers start out that way? Depressing too, many that she had read, no one ever having a happy normal childhood. Apparently Mr. Addison's book was going to follow the same pattern.

Mrs. Mercer left. She almost sneaked down the stairs, she felt so guilty over what she had done. But underneath that feeling lay a sense of relief.

But why?

Walking back to her house, looking too erect and proud to have ever stooped to prying on tenants, the answer came to Mrs. Mercer.

She felt relieved because the manuscript justified the Addisons' keeping so completely to themselves. Jay Addison really was writing a book and needed quiet and privacy to work on it. The few pages she had glanced at establishing his hero—himself, in other words—as an orphan brought up by his grandmother, probably dead by now, helped to explain his lack of family ties. Not, of course, Mrs. Addison's. Was she an orphan too? She might be. It was even possible that their aloneness was one of the things that had brought them together.

Mrs. Mercer felt easier in her mind about them as she went in her back door and was greeted by reproachful whines from Billy whose suppertime was overdue. She hadn't even realized until a few moments ago that any uneasiness at all had accompanied her praise of the couple to friends as the ideal tenants.

6

The weather at Cape Cod was perfect the whole three days of their stay, unclouded sky, ocean reflecting its blue depths, sparkling in the brilliant sunlight. Not crowded yet; without a reservation they were still able to get a room in a good beachfront motel in Truro.

Everything went along well until the second night when

Only Couples Need Apply

they drove into Provincetown to have dinner at a restaurant famed for its seafood.

Jay had three drinks to Gretchen's one in their room before they left and then two more in quick succession at the restaurant. By the time he finished his fifth drink it showed in his behavior. The bottle of wine he ordered with their meal offset whatever sobering effect food might have had on him.

Their waitress was young and pert, as dark as Gretchen was fair, voluptuous in contrast to her slimness, flaunting her body at Jay, brushing his shoulder with her breasts when she leaned forward to serve him, giving him a lingering smile each time she caught his eye.

Jay responded, returning smile for smile, consulting her at unnecessary length on what he should order, asking if she was a local girl or a college student working for the summer.

She was local, she replied, had lived all her life in Provincetown.

"College student, what a question," Gretchen said crisply when she left. "Doesn't look as if she ever got past fifth grade."

When the girl served them coffee she asked Jay—continuing to ignore Gretchen all she could—"You folks staying around here?"

"Truro," he informed her and named their motel.

Which was anything but good judgment on his part, Gretchen pointed out as they left the restaurant, her annoyance increased by the extravagant tip he gave the girl. "What happened to that hard-and-fast rule we're supposed to have, Jay?—you know, never telling anyone more than the bare minimum about ourselves."

"Oh, for God's sake, Gretchen. A dumb chick like her. What's the difference?"

"We still follow the rule," she said flatly.

She was jealous, he thought, starting the car. Gretchen always so superior, always in command, reducing him sometimes to the status of errand boy, was jealous of his little flirtation with the waitress. It had actually got under her skin, not an easy thing to do and therefore all the more pleasing to him.

But Gretchen's feelings went beyond simple jealousy. There was that, of course. Jay was her property, her lover, her escort, complementing her good looks with his own; he was the one person in the world with whom she need not keep her guard up at all times.

That side of their relationship did breed jealousy of his noticing another woman. Other feelings she had just then were centered on what she thought of as their business partnership. She was in charge of that, selecting, planning, working out every detail of their projects, but needing help to carry them out. Jay served her well in that capacity, letting her take command but playing his own part with coolest assurance when the time came for it.

Was he beginning to resent his subordinate status though? Or, another thought, had he been resenting it, at least a little bit all along?

It was possible. It was also possible that every now and then he sensed something of her deep-buried contempt for him. She tried to hide it, seldom dwelt on it herself, but it was always there just the same, bred of awareness that his talents and abilities were inferior to her own.

If she was right about this, if tonight's incident was a small signal of restiveness under her domination, he would have to be brought back into line. Especially when he drank. Although he would never admit it, he didn't have much capacity for liquor. His tongue loosened after a few drinks. That was dangerous. They couldn't afford indiscretions of any sort.

Jay had to be brought back into line . . .

She didn't mention the waitress on the way back to their motel. Her head on his shoulder, she talked about what a lovely moonlight night it was and suggested a walk on the beach before they went to bed.

The walk became a prelude to lovemaking, Gretchen wooing him, leading him on, displaying more passion and intensity than ever before. She lay awake, though, long after he was asleep, weighing in her mind their whole association and what might come of it in the future.

Although she felt tired the next morning, lying on the beach with Jay in the sun, she also felt so sure she had him securely back under her thumb that after lunch she went to their room for a nap, letting him go back out on the beach alone.

Jay settled down on a blanket and drifted off to sleep

Only Couples Need Apply 41

himself, the book he had brought along unopened beside him.

An hour later he was awakened by a teasing voice that said, "Hey, Sleeping Beauty, time you woke up."

He opened one eye and found last night's waitress on the blanket beside him, face bent over his, lips parted invitingly. It was not an invitation he was ready to refuse. He turned on his side and pulled her close to him.

Gretchen slept the afternoon away, not waking up until after five o'clock, startled then at how late it was, sitting up in bed, yawning and stretching as her gaze went around the empty room. Where was Jay—out on the beach all this time?

Their windows faced it. She went over to them, parted the curtains and looked out. The blanket and bright-jacketed paperback Jay had taken along were within her range of vision not far above the waterline as the tide came in. But Jay was nowhere in sight. Their car, parked outside their door, was gone.

Not for a single moment did Gretchen assume that he might have driven to the nearest bar or run out of cigarettes or anything like that. Last night's waitress her built-in antenna, instantly alerted, told her. She had somehow got in touch with Jay. She knew, thanks to him, where they were staying.

Gretchen fumed for the next half hour. Then she heard the car drive up outside and his knock at the door.

She flung it wide. "Oh, so you're back."

Liquor fumes, mingled with the smell of perfume, something cheap and strong, such as the waitress would use, preceded him into the room.

Gretchen sniffed disdainfully. "Someone should tell that dumb little tramp to buy better perfume."

"What dumb little—?"

"Don't bother lying. The waitress, of course. You've been with her all afternoon. What did you do—get hold of a bottle and rent a room somewhere together?"

That was what Jay and the waitress had done. He would not admit it, though; he would admit nothing except that he had got bored out there on the beach by himself and had driven to a nearby bar for a few drinks.

"Just killing time," he said over and over. "Just killing time."

"Is that the newest name for it?" Gretchen demanded scornfully. "And what did you talk about after you bedded down and had a few drinks together? Did you brag about what a gentleman of leisure you are and how much money you have? Did you tell her things that could sink in, even into her stupid head?"

That was the main issue. Not his infidelity, for all the blow that it was to her self-esteem, especially after last night's lovemaking; but what they had talked about, what he might have said to the waitress, worried her far more.

One of these days, the thought flickered through her mind, not for the first time, she might have to get rid of Jay. Success so far in their projects was making him too sure of himself. Unless he changed his attitude, it could create a real problem one of these days.

But the need to give it serious thought still lay in the future—at least she hoped so. She hoped it could wait until they had a lot more money than they had now.

She showered and dressed in stony silence. It lasted through dinner in the motel restaurant and afterward back in their room watching TV.

Jay didn't mind a fight but couldn't take the silent treatment.

"Look," he said at ten o'clock when Gretchen shut off the TV and began getting ready for bed. "Let's forget it, hon. You're making a big deal out of nothing."

She did not answer. She sat down at the dressing table to brush her hair, a silky cloud around her shoulders, gleaming in the lamplight.

"Gretchen, baby . . ." He tried to put his arms around her but she shrugged him off, eyes like gray ice meeting his in the mirror. "You were with that waitress this afternoon," she said coldly. "Why don't you stop lying about it?"

He exploded then. "All right, goddammit, I was. But it was her doing, not mine. I was asleep on the beach. She came and woke me up."

"After you encouraged her last night, going out of your way to tell her where we were staying."

"So all right, I told her. But I didn't expect her to show up here this afternoon. You were asleep. She said why didn't we go have a drink somewhere. Which we did. At the Clam Shell down the road. Three drinks altogether.

Only Couples Need Apply

Just drinks and talking about nothing. She turned out to be a drag if you really want to know. Then she had to leave for work and I had another drink by myself and came back here. That's all there was to it. No need to blow it up into a major production."

He was still lying. He wouldn't have wasted his time just sitting around a bar for three or four hours with a girl like that. Let it go, however, Gretchen decided. Keep him at his distance for a couple of days but let it go.

They left for Belmont the next morning. The weather had changed overnight, turning gray and chilly as if in keeping with the end of their holiday mood.

They arrived back at their apartment in the middle of the afternoon, Billy running to bark a greeting as they drove in just as he had barked good-by three days ago.

"Here's that damn' pest again," Jay said, getting out of the car to open the garage door. He kicked the dog, not hard, no more than a thrust of his foot to get him out of the way. But Billy gave a yelp of pain or injured feelings and darted off across the yard.

Mrs. Mercer's car was in the garage. "Better not let her see you kick Billy," Gretchen said. "He's the apple of her eye."

"Then she'd better keep him away from me," Jay retorted sharply. "Can't stand the mutt, always underfoot."

They went upstairs. "Don't touch anything until I've checked," Gretchen said.

"Oh, your little traps," Jay remarked condescendingly, but set the suitcases down near the door and waited.

Gretchen went to the desk first and opened it. "Hair's gone." She glanced into the bedroom. "Closet door's shut." The manuscript came last. "Edges all straight."

She spoke on a vindicated note. The career she had invented for Jay had now proved itself worth the time and effort involved in it. Mrs. Mercer had snooped.

"Maybe it was Billy," Jay said, giving vent to the hostility that still lingered between them.

Gretchen ignored this comment, saying in a firm voice, "There'll be more pages ready for her if she snoops again."

"The typewriter's all yours," Jay replied and carried their suitcases into the bedroom.

The phone rang while they were unpacking. Gretchen picked it up from the bedside table.

It was Mrs. Mercer, assuaging guilt feelings toward them. "Welcome home, Mrs. Addison," she said. "Did you have a good trip?"

"Fine, thank you. Just fine."

"Beautiful weather here until today. You had it on the Cape too?"

"Oh yes, Not a cloud in the sky." Gretchen paused, glancing over her shoulder at Jay. "Not until last night, that is."

"How nice for you," said Mrs. Mercer.

7

"Oh, listen to this, Jay," said Gretchen, turning to the help wanted ads in the Los Angeles *Times* as she had started doing recently.

"Alert, educated young woman as live-in companion/secretary to older woman," she read aloud. "Driver's license, typing, shorthand. References."

"Sounds good," Jay said. "Why don't you call?"

"It's a box number. I'd have to write."

They had been in Los Angeles for two months, moving from a motel into a furnished apartment on Holloway Drive off Sunset Boulevard, living high, taking expensive trips here and there as the spirit moved them.

Their apartment, new car, driver's licenses, and bank accounts were under their new names of John and Greta Wilson. Their telephone, in keeping with Gretchen's thoughts of another project as their money melted away, was listed under G. Wilson.

That morning Gretchen sat down at her rented typewriter and answered the ad.

Acknowledgment took the form of a phone call four days later.

Only Couples Need Apply 45

"May I speak to Miss Greta Wilson," said the woman who called.

"This is she speaking."

"Well, this is Mrs. Helen Atwood in Santa Barbara." The voice at the other end of the line, although fairly brisk, had a slight quaver of age. "I'd like to get together with you, Miss Wilson, to talk over your reply to my ad. Would it be an imposition to ask you to drive up here for lunch—tomorrow, say? That is, if you have a car."

"Not at all. I don't have a car of my own but I can borrow one."

"Splendid. Shall we say one o'clock? I'm at the Hotel de los Cuatro Vientos—the Four Winds Hotel in English—apartment 3-A. We'll have lunch right here."

Did she have a full-time maid? That wouldn't do at all.

Turning this possibility over in her mind, Gretchen scarcely listened to Mrs. Atwood's instructions on what exit to take off the freeway and what route to follow then to the apartment hotel. She could always find her way. A maid was a much more serious matter.

Late that afternoon Jay and Gretchen drove to Santa Barbara and located the Four Winds, a sprawling three-storied complex built in the Spanish style, white stucco, black iron balconies, arched doorways. It stood in acres of grounds on a cliff overlooking the Pacific with tennis courts and swimming pool visible in the distance.

"Super-plush," Gretchen commented as they drove up to the main entrance and circled back to the road. "Three-A," she said. "Top floor, best view, no doubt, facing the ocean."

"She must be loaded," said Jay.

"If there's a full-time maid, it's out," Gretchen said.

They went back to the motel where they had registered on their way into Santa Barbara. Wig case and suitcases were already in their room.

The next morning Gretchen dressed for her interview. Flat-heeled shoes to take away from her five-seven height, three sets of underwear to add bulk, a full pleated skirt and overblouse that added still more of it to her appearance. The only make-up she used was on her eyebrows, darkening and thickening them. Her wig of medium-brown human hair came next, a very real-looking wig that she put on carefully and pinned up in a bun in back. Last of all, she took a pair of brown-rimmed glasses out of her suitcase, put them on and studied herself in the full-length mirror.

"Well, how do I look?" she asked, turning to Jay for inspection.

"God," he said. "Just like the picture you had taken in that outfit for your driver's license. Five years older, twenty pounds fatter, at least an inch shorter—and dowdy as hell."

"Fine." Gretchen glanced at her watch. "Time to leave. Wish us luck."

"Fifty thousand dollars' worth, maybe?"

"Why not double that?" She picked up pocketbook and keys. Starting toward the door she added, "By the way, you'd better call the Downtown San Francisco Hilton while I'm gone—not from here, though—and reserve a room as of tomorrow for yourself. You're Mr. Robert Boyce, remember."

No one could walk in and out the main entrance of the Four Winds at will Gretchen discovered some twenty minutes later when she had parked in the guest parking section and gone into the lobby. The clerk at the desk gave her an inquiring look that drew her in his direction.

"May I help you?"

"Miss Wilson to see Mrs. Atwood."

"If you'll just wait a moment ..." He turned to a switchboard, turned back after a murmur of inquiry and waved her on. "The elevators are just around the corner to your right, Miss Wilson."

"Thank you," Gretchen took her time moving with the heavy-footed gait she had adopted to suit her disguise, looking around, spotting a big youngish man reading a magazine at the far side of the lobby, cataloguing him as a house detective, security guard, or whatever title the hotel assigned to him.

There were two elevators manned by operators, a further screening of undesirables.

"Third, please," she said, stepping into the nearer one, her thoughts still on the layout of the hotel. There would be stairways, too, of course, and service elevators. Anyone living here would soon find ways of going in and out freely without running the gauntlet of the lobby.

Mrs. Atwood met her at the door of her apartment, a

Only Couples Need Apply

small birdlike woman somewhere in her middle seventies. Her clothes were expensive but she looked almost as dowdy as Gretchen did. She wore too much jewelry, a sapphire brooch pinned on crookedly, matching earrings, and two or three diamond rings on each hand.

"So kind of you to come all this way to see me, Miss Wilson," she began. "I hope you had no trouble finding the place." She went on in that vein for another moment or two as if Los Angeles were a hundred miles away and the hotel situated in the middle of a trackless desert with no landmarks or signposts leading to it.

A nonstop talker, Gretchen thought. She made polite noises, following her prospective employer through a spacious foyer into an enormous living room with a wood-burning fireplace and a wall of windows across the front commanding a view of the ocean. A beautiful room—someday she would have one like it, Gretchen told herself—furnished with early Spanish pieces and dim old paintings.

Mrs. Atwood gestured to a deep sofa facing the windows and offered a choice of drinks.

"A daiquiri, please," Gretchen said primly but not overdoing the primness in case Mrs. Atwood turned out to be a lush.

When she had made the drinks Mrs. Atwood carried hers, a martini, over to the telephone. "Let me just order lunch sent up and then we can settle down and get acquainted, Miss Wilson."

She put on the glasses that hung from a chain around her neck and picked up the menu on the telephone table.

"Shrimp Scampi today, I see. If you like shrimp, they do it very well here. Not too much garlic, subtle flavor—"

"Sounds fine," Gretchen replied.

"Avocado salad—"

"Whatever you say, Mrs. Atwood."

Mrs. Atwood pressed a button on the phone and began giving their order, fussing about wine, going on to what kind of rolls they had today, those divine little hard ones, she hoped, with lots of sweet butter. Something light for dessert—what fresh fruits were there?

Meals sent up, maid service furnished by the hotel, thought Gretchen. No need for Mrs. Atwood to have a maid of her own.

They had another cocktail while they waited for lunch. Mrs. Atwood's faded blue eyes taking in every detail of Gretchen's solid, reliable spinsterish appearance—not likely to rush off and get married just when they got used to each other—and finding satisfactory the answers she had ready for every question.

She came from Pittsburgh, Pennsylvania, she said. She was employed there for several years by the late Mrs. Walter Boyce as a companion. After Mrs. Boyce's death three months ago she had moved to Los Angeles where her only relative, a cousin she had grown up with, lived.

Her educational background? An associate degree in secretarial science, she said, naming a junior college in Vermont.

Mrs. Atwood wrote it down but Gretchen felt reasonably confident she would not check it, inconveniently far off as it was. If she did, there'd be no job but that was a chance worth taking.

Gretchen gave the name of Robert Boyce, her late employer's son, as a reference.

"I called him yesterday after I talked with you, Mrs. Atwood," she said. "He told me he was leaving today for San Francisco—he makes a lot of business trips—and that if you wanted to write or call him he has a reservation at the Downtown Hilton and will be there for the rest of the week."

Mrs. Atwood wrote that down too. "Any previous references?" she inquired.

Gretchen shook her head. She had added three years to her age, saying she was thirty. Seven years with the fictitious Mrs. Boyce, two years before that taking care of the aunt who had reared her orphaned self in her last illness. It was all airtight—as long as Mrs. Atwood did not check her educational background.

There was a knock at the door. A waiter wheeled in their lunch, served it on a table in the dining ell and departed.

Over lunch Mrs. Atwood talked at tedious length about the Society for the Preservation of Historic Spanish Landmarks in Southern California of which, it developed, she was president.

"So much correspondence," she said. "That's why I need a companion who can also double as a secretary. Right

Only Couples Need Apply

now, for example, we're working hard to raise funds for the restoration of Nuestra Señora de las Sierras, an old mission church dating back to the seventeenth century. When it was brought to our attention two years ago it was in terrible condition, boarded up, about to be torn down to make a parking lot. Imagine, Miss Wilson! We managed to get together the money to buy it and we're hoping to get started on the restoration soon . . ."

Gretchen, looking alert and interested, closed her ears as she went on talking about the church until they finished lunch.

Mrs. Atwood then asked her if she would mind taking a letter and typing it. "Of course I've already seen a sample of your typing in your reply to my ad but still, if you don't mind—?"

"No indeed," said Gretchen.

Mrs. Atwood took her to a small room equipped as an office with filing cabinets and an electric typewriter. Her pleasure in the finished product made Gretchen feel that the job was virtually hers.

This was what she reported back to Jay an hour later. "She's hooked," she said. "Asked if a starting salary of a hundred a week plus room, board and laundry would be satisfactory. Wanted to know if I'd ever driven a hand shift Mercedes. Showed me the room and bath I'd have in the rear of the apartment."

Gretchen paused. "Looks like a good setup, Jay. No children, no close relatives to drop by unexpectedly. Must have tons of money, too, the way she lives. She seemed quite taken with me. I could read her mind as she saw me to the door and I clumped off. Good dowdy character, no dates, nobody about to whisk me off to the altar."

Gretchen paused again. She never smiled much but now she gave him one of her rare smiles, a sleek contented one. "So that's it," she said. "I'll drive you to the airport and you hop the next flight to San Francisco. You got a reservation at the Hilton all right?"

"Yes."

"Well then, you just wait for her to call you."

"What do you want me to say?" Jay, stretched out on his bed, watched Gretchen whisk out of her costume and wig and emerge from the bathroom her usual elegant self.

"Dependable, conscientious, devoted to your mother,

that's what you'll say," she told him. "Don't make it too glowing, though. You're a businessman. You visited your mother as often as you could but generally felt that she was in capable hands."

Late that afternoon Gretchen dropped him off at the airport booked for a flight to San Francisco. Still later, around ten that evening, he called her from the Hilton.

"Just heard from your Mrs. Atwood," he said. "You're all set, I guess."

"Unless she writes to Vermont. You'd better stay put another day or two, though, in case she calls again."

But instead, two days later Mrs. Atwood called Gretchen.

"How soon could you start in here with me, Miss Wilson?" she asked.

It was a Thursday. "Monday, Mrs. Atwood?"

"That will be fine. I'll expect you sometime Monday morning."

Gretchen called Jay in San Francisco. "You can come back now," she said. "The project is launched."

8

They got on well together. It took Gretchen far less time than she had expected to install herself in Mrs. Atwood's good graces.

Studying the older woman, listening to her flow of reminiscences, she soon understood why. Mrs. Atwood, open and trusting by nature, insulated by money from the harsher realities of life, had always been quick to take people at their face value. Her husband, it seemed, had tried to restrain this impulsive trait. But he was dead now and there was no one else, no other guiding hand, in his place.

Other factors entered into it. Mrs. Atwood was beginning to feel her age, seeking a substitute for her lack of family ties. She needed someone to lean on; someone who would look after her, remind her of appointments and obligations, take her wherever she wanted to go; and, above all, keep her company, give her the reassurance of another human presence in her big empty apartment.

Once Gretchen had taken Mrs. Atwood's measure, she found it no problem to satisfy these basic needs. She took over all her correspondence—most of it, she noted, dealing with the historical society, with little that was personal—put her helter-skelter files in order, paid the household bills and generally fulfilled all the requirements of a competent secretary.

She functioned equally well as a companion, making a fourth at bridge, driving Mrs. Atwood everywhere she wanted to go—Mrs. Atwood, she learned, still had a driver's license but had lost confidence in herself after a freeway accident a year ago—watching her favorite TV programs with her, playing gin rummy by the hour, helping entertain her small circle of friends, tireless in her efforts to fill every vacant corner of her life.

By midwinter Gretchen had made herself so indispensable that Mrs. Atwood began telling everyone that Gretchen was more like a daughter than a paid companion, that she couldn't imagine how she had ever got along without her.

While Mrs. Atwood sang her praises, Gretchen, making out checks for her to sign, going to her banks to make deposits or withdrawals, acquainted herself with every detail of her employer's financial situation.

Somewhere around twenty thousand in her checking account at all times, she told Jay. About twenty-five thousand in two separate savings accounts. This money and her jewelry, kept in a wall safe in her bedroom, constituted her liquid assets.

"Her real income is from a trust fund left by her husband," she said. "Nearly a hundred thousand a year after taxes but she spends it like water."

"Even so, a pretty good haul counting her jewelry," said Jay.

He bought himself a brown wig and glasses before he made his first visit to the apartment to take Gretchen out to dinner. Introduced as Gretchen's cousin John, Mrs. Atwood, looking at the wig and glasses, immediately detected a family resemblance between them.

In her warmhearted way, she was prepared to make much of him, dear Greta's only relative, but this did not suit Jay and Gretchen's purposes. His visits lessened, gradually ceased, Gretchen meeting him somewhere else on her afternoons off. In the meantime, though, Jay had been accepted by the staff as a legitimate visitor and learned how to find his way in and out of the hotel by side entrances.

"Soon now," Gretchen said to him one day early in March. "I've had all I can take of the stupid old bitch and her stupid old Spanish landmarks. What about the gun?"

"I'll buy it this week."

"Let's make it next week then. Whatever day she decides we're going to stay home all day and work out schedules for the fund drive in May. Tuesday, probably. I'll call and let you know."

They were at their apartment. Jay got to his feet, walked over to the window and stood looking out. "Just the money and the jewelry," he said on a dissatisfied note.

"Yes."

He turned to face her. "Christ, some of the stuff in that place is worth a small fortune."

"You thinking of taking the Goya maybe? Or the Picasso drawing? Or the Georgian silver service? You won't have room for them in your cell."

He eyed her sullenly. There she was, being all smart-ass and superior again. Sometimes he felt like wringing her neck, that lovely proud neck that no disguise could hide . . .

"There's other stuff," he muttered. "Lots of it."

"No," she said incisively. "Just the money and the jewelry." She stood up. "Time I got back."

That night she began wiping off her fingerprints every chance she had. In her own room and bath she began wearing gloves.

She called Jay the following Tuesday morning. "The maid's here now," she said. "But take your time, an hour, say, and she'll be gone."

Mrs. Atwood, making a leisurely start on her day, was in her room, just finishing getting dressed, when he arrived.

Gretchen led the way to it and opened the door.

"Why, John, what are you doing here?" Mrs. Atwood wheeled around from her mirror in surprise and displea-

Only Couples Need Apply

sure over the intrusion. "There's been no call from the desk to announce—" Her voice faltered as she saw the gun in his gloved hand. "Greta . . . ?"

Gretchen said nothing, eyes blank behind her glasses.

"Just take it easy, Mrs. Atwood," Jay said advancing into the room. "Real easy." Then he let Gretchen tell her why he was there.

She wouldn't believe it at first. They had to allow several minutes for her outraged protests and exclamations, her reproaches to Gretchen. They made no reply. They just stood there in front of her, as indifferent to anything she said as the cliff beyond the windows to the sea pounding at its base.

Their silence was as frightening as the gun.

Gretchen left the room and came back with the passbooks for her two savings accounts and a check for fifteen thousand dollars made out to cash.

"Just sign this, Mrs. Atwood," she said.

Mrs. Atwood looked at her dear Greta's face that had become the face of a stranger and signed.

"Now these," Gretchen said, opening the passbooks to hand her forms copied from them authorizing withdrawals from one account of eight thousand dollars and twelve thousand from the other.

Mrs. Atwood signed them.

Jay stepped forward to read the figures over her shoulder.

"Why not more?" he asked Gretchen.

"Questions, maybe, if we cut too close to the bone."

They talked over Mrs. Atwood's head as if she weren't there.

"Now, Mrs. Atwood, call the three banks and tell them I'm on my way to make the withdrawals in cash."

It was like a rerun of the Sherman project, Gretchen thought. Except that Mrs. Atwood had not had a stroke, had nothing wrong with her heart and would not oblige them by dying of shock over what was happening to her.

Instead, it had numbed her. She sat there like a zombie doing what she was told.

"Don't try to pull anything when you talk to the banks," Gretchen continued. "If any questions are asked about wanting cash, cut them off. It's your money, remember.

You have a right to draw it out whatever way you please."

The calls were made between swallows from the glass of water Gretchen had brought her.

"Very good," Gretchen said at the end. "Nothing to worry about now as long as you behave yourself. John will stay here with you while I'm gone. If the phone rings answer it in case it's some sort of question from one of the banks. If it's not that, just say you're on your way out and you'll call back later. Have you got it all straight, Mrs. Atwood?"

"Yes."

"Well then, remember there's nothing to worry about. It's only money and with all you've got you'll never really miss it."

It went like clockwork just as it had on the Sherman project. Gretchen took the elevator to the basement garage and exchanged pleasantries with the man in charge while an attendant drove Mrs. Atwood's Mercedes out to the ramp.

It didn't even take long. Gretchen was back, the money in a leather briefcase she had made it a point to carry in and out with her recently, soon after one o'clock.

"How's it gone?" she asked Jay.

"No problems. One phone call from some character in the historical society but Mrs. Atwood handled it just fine. She asked for brandy and I gave it to her. Had some myself. Good for my nerves too." He grinned at their victim. "Right, old girl?"

Mrs. Atwood said nothing. She thought her ordeal was nearly over as she watched Gretchen—her dear Greta!—get the key to her safe, take out her jewelry and put it in the briefcase.

"The rings you're wearing," Gretchen said.

Mrs. Atwood, huddled in her chair, handed them over.

"We ready to take off now?" Jay asked.

"No," said Gretchen. "Fingerprints."

She put on a pair of gloves and moved from room to room wiping them off every surface where they might be found, taking her time, her task made easier by the maid's daily cleaning and the care she had taken herself these past few days.

Her Greta Wilson clothes would be left behind—she

couldn't afford to draw attention to herself carrying out suitcases—but it didn't matter. They had all come from the bargain basements of Los Angeles stores and couldn't be traced.

"God, it's taking you forever," Jay said when she finally returned to the bedroom. The strain was beginning to tell on him, Gretchen saw. "Better to be safe than sorry, isn't it?" she replied with deliberate coolness and proceeded to wipe off every surface in that room too.

At last it was done.

"That's it," she said, giving Jay a warning glance because his face looked too taut and dangerous now, his eyes much too bright.

She turned to their victim. "Time to tie you up," she said.

"No!" Mrs. Atwood sprang to her feet. "There's no need of it. You've done enough to me already, betraying my trust in you, robbing me at the point of a gun—"

"Be reasonable, Mrs. Atwood." Gretchen spoke quietly, soothingly, as to a child. "We've got to have the time to get away. If we left you free, you'd be on the phone to the police before we could get out of the hotel."

After a moment of resistance Mrs. Atwood allowed herself to be pressed back down onto the chair again. Her brief flare of protest was ended, her helplessness against these two once more uppermost in her mind.

Gretchen went over to the bureau and got out a handful of nylon stockings.

"You tie her up," she said to Jay.

He handed her the gun. She kept it trained on Mrs. Atwood while he tied her up, hands behind her back, feet together, a rope of stockings fastening her to the chair and last of all, one whipped into her mouth and knotted at the back of her head.

Gretchen gave him back the gun and walked across the room to turn on the bedside radio, twirling the knob until she found a station blasting out hard rock.

Mrs. Atwood's eyes widened in horror as the reason for the cacophony, the only possible one, struck home to her. A muffled cry burst through her gag, she tried to get up...

"Now," said Gretchen, turning the volume still higher.

Jay, his eyes even brighter than before, moved around behind Mrs. Atwood and fired a bullet into the back of her head as she made a last frantic effort to twist away from him.

"Jesus, look at that." His fascinated gaze was fixed on the raw bleeding wound he had made.

"Look at your shirt front," Gretchen said, turning off the radio. "Better wash the blood off it right away before it has a chance to dry."

"I will," he said, but still stood there while Gretchen went around in front of Mrs. Atwood and with fastidious touch raised the sagging head to look at the dead face, eyes bulging from their sockets.

"Just to be sure," she said.

"God, how could there be any doubt about it?" Jay hurried into the bathroom to wash off his shirt front.

"Use cold water," Gretchen called after him.

It took him only a few moments to get the stains out. When he put on his jacket and buttoned it up, none of the wet spots showed.

He slipped the gun inside his waistband. "Let's get out of here," he said.

Gretchen picked up the briefcase and her pocketbook.

"Where did you leave your car?" she asked as she followed him out of the room.

"Near the entrance."

"All right, you go first," Gretchen said. "I'll be down in a few minutes. Oh, but you haven't told me what kind of a car you rented after you sold ours yesterday."

"Green Ford," Jay opened the hall door, saw no one and slipped out, heading for the stairway at the far end of the corridor.

Gretchen took a DO NOT DISTURB card out of a chest in the foyer and hung it outside on the doorknob as she left. There was still no one in sight. She checked to make sure the door was locked and then proceeded without haste to the elevator.

She greeted the elevator operator with the sedateness befitting a paid companion, nodded to the desk clerk on her way through the lobby and said yes, it was a lovely day to a fellow resident she passed on the steps outside.

Jay was waiting in the green Ford around the corner from the underground garage. Gretchen gave a last fleeting thought to the Mercedes. Nothing to worry about there. She'd had it washed yesterday, wiped it off inside wherever she might have left fingerprints and worn gloves driving back to the hotel.

They lost no time getting to the motel near the freeway where Jay had stayed last night. The bag Gretchen had packed to be kept separate from the rest of her luggage was in his room. Twenty minutes later, leaving the motel, no one from the Four Winds would have recognized her as Mrs. Atwood's dowdy, brown-haired companion. Or Jay, without his wig and glasses, as her cousin John.

The gun went into one paper bag to be disposed of in a trash can, the bullets into another.

Late that night they landed at O'Hare Airport in Chicago.

9

They had dinner with Mrs. Mercer the week after their trip to Cape Cod. There was no way to avoid the invitation when she gave them a choice of nights and knew their social life was nonexistent.

"No other guests," she said. "Just the three of us."

At least there was that, Gretchen said, no other guests to ask questions, study them at close quarters. Jay, with his own private plans in mind, raised no objections at all.

They dressed up for the occasion in clothes bought earlier that week in the most expensive shops in Belmont. Gretchen wore a hand-screened linen dress, Jay a green-and-blue-striped Pierre Cardin shirt with a charcoal green silk suit.

They crossed the yard to Mrs. Mercer's at six o'clock. There was no need to go around to the front door. She came out onto the back porch as they approached.

"I thought we'd have drinks out here on the terrace," she said.

The flagstone terrace, comfortably furnished and shaded by a maple tree, was at the far side of the back porch. An ice bucket and bottles of liquor and mixes already stood on a low table. Mrs. Mercer let Jay make their drinks while she brought out an assortment of hors d'oeuvres.

When they were seated, Jay's eyes strayed to Mrs. Mercer's diamond bracelet. Heirloom, he thought from its old-fashioned style. God, every time he saw the woman she was wearing different pieces of jewelry. Never too much of it at a time but always something valuable. The diamonds in that bracelet, for instance, must be between two and three carats each.

When he had finished his first drink he said, "May I use your bathroom, Mrs. Mercer?"

"Certainly. First door to your left going into the front hall from the kitchen."

Her keys were his objective. He tried them out, one ear cocked toward the terrace, and discovered that the same one fitted front and back doors. He slipped it off its hook and put it in his pocket.

After he had made a second round of drinks he brought out his cigarettes and exclaimed ruefully, "Lord, only one left."

"Smoke mine," said Mrs. Mercer.

"Thank you, not my brand. Nor Gretchen's. She smokes mentholated."

Gretchen raised her eyebrows. "Didn't you buy a carton only three or four days ago?"

"Let's not talk about how much I smoke." He set down his drink. "Will you ladies excuse me while I run over to the shopping center and pick some up?"

"Yes, of course," Mrs. Mercer said. Gretchen gave him a puzzled look, almost certain that he still had cigarettes left at home.

Jay drove to the shopping plaza, bought a carton of cigarettes and went into the hardware store to have a duplicate key made from the one in his pocket. It took an extra ten minutes.

"Drugstore was mobbed," he said when he got back. "Thought I'd never get out of there."

"Well, we're a drink ahead of you now," Mrs. Mercer said. "Make yourself another while I check on dinner."

"You're smoking much too much if that carton you bought the other day is gone," Gretchen said when they were alone.

Only Couples Need Apply

"Don't lecture, darling. Have another shrimp." He passed the bowl to her.

Mrs. Mercer brought up Jay's book during dinner. "How's it coming, Mr. Addison?" she inquired.

"Not too fast," he replied. "I'm new at it, you know."

"Well, yes, that must make a difference." Mrs. Mercer paused. "By the way, a man you might enjoy meeting will be at his cottage here next month. He's a writer, too, mostly magazine articles, I think, but I'm sure you'd have a lot in common."

That's very nice of you, Mrs. Mercer, but I'd rather not," Jay said, his tone abrupt, almost brusque.

Gretchen intervened. "Maybe another time," she said. "Jay's not ready to talk to an established writer yet. Besides, we are playing hermit this summer, you know, to keep him from distractions."

Mrs. Mercer dropped the subject. Presently Gretchen got her talking about Belmont, the changes she had seen as the town grew with the suburban sprawl long since spread out over what had once been farmland belonging to her late husband's people.

No wonder she was loaded, thought Jay, looking at her diamond bracelet again.

When Mrs. Mercer suggested they have liqueurs out on the terrace he stayed behind—there was always the bathroom for an excuse—and put her house key back where it belonged.

On his way out he paused at the back door to try the duplicate key he'd had made. Sometimes they didn't come out quite right but this one fitted the lock perfectly. He had no idea yet as to when he would have a chance to use it but he liked having it in his possession. He particularly liked having put something over on Gretchen in getting it.

They stayed for another hour, the conversation moving along easily.

What a charming young couple they were, Mrs. Mercer reflected after they left. She had really enjoyed having them over.

And yet ...

She thought about the evening, little things about it that had brought back the faint uneasiness over her tenants dispelled by seeing Jay Addison's manuscript.

One thing that seemed strange was his refusal to meet a

fellow writer. Even more strange, perhaps, was their reticence the whole evening about themselves. None of the usual reminiscences, anecdotes about relatives or friends or places they had been, nothing at all, in fact, that revealed anything about their background.

They had every right, of course, to keep their private affairs to themselves if they wanted to. But still ...

The next morning Gretchen copied four pages from the book instead of two. Just in case, she told Jay, Mrs. Mercer decided to come snooping again.

Jay was unconcerned. If she did, he doubted that her snooping would extend to looking under the lining paper of his top bureau drawer. That was where he had hidden her house key.

There was no way for them to know that Mrs. Mercer hadn't the least intention of ever invading their privacy again.

But Jay intended to invade hers—at the right time, under the right conditions.

These entailed the absence of Mrs. Mercer and Gretchen for a minimum of an hour or more after dark. Mrs. Mercer went our fairly often in the evening; Gretchen by herself only when she did the laundry at night following her practice of varying times and places for doing it.

He had to wait nearly a month for his opportunity. It came at the end of a July day when they had spent the afternoon at the beach and then gone out for an early dinner after Gretchen said it was too hot to cook. They got home shortly before eight just in time to see Mrs. Mercer get into her car.

"Well, you look very nice tonight," Gretchen remarked, eyeing the sleeveless yellow dress that set off Mrs. Mercer's deep tan while Jay eyed the topaz pin she wore with it. "Special occasion?"

"Not really, Mrs. Addison. Just a bridge party." She started her car and drove off.

"You know, it seems to be getting a bit cooler," Gretchen said on their way upstairs. "I think I'll go to the laundromat tonight instead of waiting until tomorrow. It's going to be hot again, the weather report said."

"Want me to go with you?"

Only Couples Need Apply

It was safe to ask. She never did. They were more noticeable together, she said.

This ultracautious attitude of hers sometimes annoyed Jay—no need of it, he said, here in Belmont, where they were far away from the locale of any of their projects—but tonight it was just what he wanted.

He helped her gather up the laundry, carried the bulging bag downstairs to the car and smiled with satisfaction as she drove away out of sight.

Both of them accounted for now, he had the place to himself. Wait a little while for it to begin getting dark and he'd be all set.

But he reckoned without Billy curled up outside Mrs. Mercer's back door, jumping up, barking wildly as Jay started up the steps.

"Shut up," he snapped, cuffing the dog on the head.

It was the wrong move. Billy, not used to being hit, expressed his outrage by snarling and nipping at Jay's heels.

Jesus, why hadn't he made friends with the mutt instead of keeping him at his distance?

He cuffed Billy harder. The dog went into a frenzy of barking and lunged at his leg. Jay lost all self-control and dealt him a vicious karate chop that sent him flying off the porch onto the cement landing below.

Jay stared at the furry little huddle for a moment, then ran down the steps for a closer look. The dog was dead, his neck broken.

"God," he muttered to himself.

He poked the limp form with his foot. "What the hell do I do about it?"

He shoved the duplicate key back into his pocket and dropped down on the bottom step, all thought of going into the house driven out of his mind by the need to cope with the dog's body.

He lit a cigarette and smoked it slowly, flicking the ashes into his cupped hand, pinching out the butt and walking across the yard to throw it into the shrubbery. Back then to the porch, pausing beside the body, poking it once more with his foot, scowling the while.

What to do with it? Wrap it in something, put it in the car when Gretchen got back and dump it out somewhere by the roadside?

No. Not tell Gretchen at all. Or have Mrs. Mercer raising a great fuss over the disappearance of her pet.

Something, though, something. Couldn't just leave it there. Not a hope that she would think it had fallen down the steps and broken its neck.

Presently the solution came to him, obvious, simple. Carry it out front and dump it in the street. Hit by a car, a glancing blow that flung it against the curb and broke its neck. Not a mark on it. Just somebody's fender, the dog maybe chasing the car—did Billy chase cars?—and head-shakes over people who hit animals and didn't even stop to report it or look for the owner.

Jay picked up the dog by his collar, held the dangling little body away from him and carried it down the driveway. He waited in the shelter of a hemlock tree until a car went by and there were no others in sight in either direction. He walked up the street then past a slight curve that would shield the body from Gretchen's headlights and dropped it against the curb.

Striking his hands together in a symbolic gesture of brushing them off—although there was nothing to brush off—Jay went home, his foray at Mrs. Mercer's postponed.

He was watching TV when Gretchen returned and went downstairs to help her carry up the clean laundry.

"How I hate laundromats," she said while she was putting it away. "Make me a drink, will you? I'm just about dead."

It put Jay on the defensive. "You've been saying all along you didn't want to send it out," he reminded her heading for the kitchen.

"You know why." She kicked off her sandals and rubbed her bare feet together. "You know we don't want a regular laundryman coming in here every week getting a good chance to look us over."

Jay didn't answer. Gretchen's trips to the laundromat were about the only time he ever had to himself.

"Let's watch the late movie," she said when he came back into the living room with their drinks. "Forget what it is but it looked pretty good."

He would have preferred being in bed with the lights out when Mrs. Mercer got home—she kept Billy in at night and would start looking for him right away—but

Only Couples Need Apply

didn't want to make an issue of it. They often watched the late movie these leisurely summer nights and if he said he was going to bed Gretchen would stay up anyway.

They heard Mrs. Mercer drive in not long before midnight. She would see their lights on and call a little later when she couldn't find Billy, Jay thought.

He got to his feet the moment the phone rang. "I'll get it. Probably a wrong number this time of night."

It was Mrs. Mercer, apologetic over disturbing them but wanting to know if they had seen Billy around that evening.

"I've called and called and he hasn't come," she said worriedly. "It's very unusual. I've trained him not to leave the yard and he's always waiting for me at the back door when I get home. I can't imagine what's become of him."

"I haven't seen him myself, Mrs. Mercer, but wait a minute and I'll ask my wife. She was out for a while."

He put the phone down and went to the living-room door. "It's Mrs. Mercer, Gretchen. She can't find her dog. Was he around when you came in?"

"I didn't see him," Gretchen replied.

Jay returned to the phone to report this. "Maybe Billy just took off somewhere," he suggested. "You know, a nice summer night and all."

"He never does that."

"But he must have tonight if he's not in the yard," Jay pointed out, warming to his role of innocent bystander.

"Well, thank you, anyway," Mrs. Mercer said, "I'll go back out now and start looking for him again."

"I hope you find him," said Jay and hung up.

He returned to his chair. "I'll make us another drink," he said. "Maybe I should go out first, though, and offer to help look for Billy. You know, neighborly."

"Up to you," Gretchen looked surprised that he would bother.

"Be right back," he said.

He heard Mrs. Mercer calling, "Here Billy ... Come, Billy," as he opened the door.

She was out in front of her house. A neighbor across the street had just started over to her.

"Have you seen Billy tonight, Jim?" she asked the neighbor as Jay approached. "He was on the back porch when I left. He's so good about staying in the yard—I just can't understand—"

The neighbor hadn't seen him. "Except early, around six o'clock."

"Oh, Mr. Addison." Mrs. Mercer turned to greet Jay. "I don't think you've met my neighbor, Mr. Jackman. Mr. Addison, Jim."

They nodded to each other.

"Thought I might help you look, Mrs. Mercer," said Jay. "You go one way and I'll go the other. Billy can't be too far away. Maybe he's found a girl friend around here somewhere."

"Can't be that. He was altered years ago. Little scamp must have started chasing a cat or something. He'll get a good scolding from me when I find him."

"Well, I'll go this way." Jay turned in the opposite direction from where he had left the body and began calling, "Here, Billy. Here, Billy . . ."

"As long as you've got help, Anna, I'll go along home." The neighbor headed back across the street.

Before he reached his house he was stopped short by Mrs. Mercer's anguished cry, "Oh, my God! Oh, Billy!"

Jay, waiting to hear it, rushed back to her but the neighbor, who was closer, got there first and found her crouched over the forlorn little heap at the curb.

He knelt beside her, touched the stiffening body, said gently, "There's nothing you can do for him, Anna," and drew her to her feet.

She burst into tears. "Oh, what could have happened to the poor little fellow?"

Jay bent over the body. "A car," he said straightening up.

The neighbor knelt again and raised the dog's head. "Neck's broken. Probably only a glancing blow from the car—don't seem to be any other injuries—but it threw him against the curb and that did it." He stood up. "At least, Anna, it was quick. Try to take some comfort from that."

But Mrs. Mercer was inconsolable. "I got him as a puppy nearly five years ago. Such good company ever since, so affectionate, slept at the foot of my bed—"

Broken phrases of grief poured from her as they took her home, the neighbor assuring her that he'd take care of the body, get a box, a blanket, bury Billy in the morning. "You pick the spot, Anna . . ."

"Maybe I can give you a hand," Jay said, playing his role to the hilt now.

"Your wife home?" the neighbor asked in an undertone as Mrs. Mercer went weeping up the back steps ahead of them. "Mine's away. Might help if there was a woman."

"I'll get Gretchen."

Jay hurried back to the apartment and told her what had happened.

"Just stay with Mrs. Mercer a few minutes while we're taking care of the dog. Make her a drink maybe. The way she's carrying on, you'd think someone in her family died."

"Well . . ." Gretchen stood up reluctantly. "Let's cut it as short as we can. And not get mixed up with this neighbor any more than we have to, either."

Mrs. Mercer was sitting at the kitchen table when they went in her back door.

Gretchen adopted a sympathetic expression. "I'm so sorry, Mrs. Mercer. A car, Jay said."

"It might at least have stopped," wept Mrs. Mercer. "At least tried to do something. I can't imagine what made Billy run out into the street, anyway. He was taught not to . . . His collar, Jim. I'd like to keep it."

"Yes, Anna."

Jay followed the neighbor across the street to his house where he found a cardboard carton in the basement and rummaged out an old blanket.

He brought along a flashlight and examined the body carefully before he wrapped it in the blanket, removing the collar first, and laid it in the box.

"Could have managed alone, I guess," he told Jay. "Billy, poor little tyke, wasn't a very big dog."

"I'll carry him," Jay said, picking up the box and taking it to the garage.

As it turned out, there was no way not to get mixed up with the neighbor; he went back to Mrs. Mercer's with Jay. Gretchen had made them both a drink and Mrs. Mercer urged the two men to have one too. Another half hour went by before they all left, the neighbor still shaking his head over the way Billy had been killed, not a mark or a cut, not even a scrape on his body, just the broken neck.

"It was sort of funny at that," Gretchen remarked going back to the apartment. "You'd think even a bumper or a fender would leave a mark somewhere."

"For God's sake, don't you start on that too," Jay said impatiently. "Let's just drop it, huh? Getting like a broken record."

Gretchen gave him a quick measuring look and dropped it. But getting ready for bed she asked, "You go out at all while I was at the laundromat?"

"No, I didn't. Just watched TV. Why?"

She thought there was a note half-belligerent, half-defensive in his voice. But it was no use pursuing the subject. If Jay knew anything about the dog's death—although how could he?—he would not admit it. It didn't matter anyway. What was one dog more or less in the world?

By the time they got up the next morning Billy was already buried in the spot Mrs. Mercer had chosen near her rose garden. The neighbor, they learned later, had dug the grave before he left for work.

Jay helped her pile stones on it that afternoon.

"So kind of you," Mrs. Mercer said wiping away tears.

10

Cora Engels was a drag, timid, colorless, self-effacing, not even, except for her last defiant gesture, worth talking about afterward as far as Gretchen and Jay were concerned.

People who knew her well saw her in a different light, pathetic, adrift in widowhood, after years of being completely overshadowed by her husband, a dynamic figure in the automotive industry, an autocratic figure at home.

She lived alone after his death in their big secluded house in Birmingham, a Detroit suburb, with only daily help coming in twice a week and few resources within herself to shorten the long empty days.

Only Couples Need Apply

At last in her desperate loneliness she listened to a friend who said, "What you need, Cora, is a companion..."

She advertised for one in the Detroit *Free Press* a few weeks after Gretchen and Jay, returning from a month's vacation in Hawaii, settled into a furnished apartment in Chicago and began buying out-of-town newspapers.

Gretchen answered the ad promptly giving her name as Geraldine Cooper, her address as the Dearborn Street YWCA where she had rented a room to make token use of a week ago.

It was as reassuring an address to sixty-seven-year-old Mrs. Engels as it was meant to be. A young woman of twenty-eight, living in the YWCA without close family ties, expressing a readiness to move to the Detroit area seemed just what she was looking for. There was the letter, too, impeccably written, educational background given as an associate degree in secretarial science from a junior college in Vermont—she would surely be able to keep Mrs. Engels's muddled household accounts and bank statements in order—and a generally agreeable tone that pleased her prospective employer.

She didn't sound like one of these modern young things in mini-skirts with long hair and brash manners; or, moving into a new city, apt to have boy friends calling her at all hours.

Mrs. Engels replied to the letter the day she received it, giving it priority over two others that came in the same mail, both from older women looking for a comfortable home and probably not at all what Mrs. Engels sought in a companion, wanting, as she did, someone much younger to bring a breath of life into the house.

Gretchen, once more dowdily dressed, wearing a new black wig and black-framed glasses flew to Detroit at Mrs. Engels's expense for an interview.

The house looked promising as she drove up in a taxi, a big house that spelled money, separated from its neighbors by two or three acres of grounds.

In no time, she took Mrs. Engels's measure, her aloneness, dependent personality, vulnerability, eagerness to win approval. No live-in help, signs of affluence everywhere.

It would do for their next project.

A week later Gretchen moved in and took up her duties as Mrs. Engels's companion.

All too soon, though, she learned that the project wasn't going to live up to her expectations. Not that much jewelry, she reported to Jay, not the large bank balances she had hoped for.

"Nothing like Mrs. Atwood's," she said. "Money tied up, never any more than twelve to fifteen thousand altogether in checking and savings accounts."

"Not worth making a real production of," said Jay discontentedly.

"No. We'll just cut and run with what we can."

They killed Mrs. Engels the second week of August following the same procedure they had used with Mrs. Atwood. This time, however, it wasn't quite so easy.

At first it seemed that it would be, Mrs. Engels stunned, terrorized by the gun, making phone calls to her banks, Gretchen off to withdraw the money, Jay left standing guard.

Trouble came near the end through a phone call.

"If its not your bank, say you'll call back," Jay said, picking up the receiver and handing it to her.

Mrs. Engels did as she was told. "Oh, Alice, I can't talk now," she said. "I'll call you back later and we can fix things up then for our bridge game tomorrow."

Gretchen, returning right after she hung up, whisked around the room wiping off last-minute fingerprints while Jay dumped Mrs. Engels's jewelry into the briefcase with the money.

"Car's taken care of," she said. "Everything okay here?"

"Well, there was a phone call from some friend just before you got back. No problem, though. Mrs. Engels said she'd call her back later about their bridge game tomorrow."

"Bridge game?" Gretchen spun around to their victim, hunched in a chair, and slapped her hard across the face. "You bitch, you miserable double-crossing bitch," she exclaimed. And to Jay, "She doesn't even know how to play bridge. Imagine it, a mouse like her, a worm, trying to screw us up!"

"Holy Christ."

"Kill her now, Jay, this very minute. We've got to get out of here before anyone shows up."

Only Couples Need Apply   69

Mrs. Engels screamed, started to get to her feet. Jay shot her twice, one bullet going too high, the other through the heart. The impact knocked her flat, her chair landing on top of her. Her mouth opened. Blood ran out of it as she died.

Gretchen grabbed the briefcase. Jay dashed out of the house ahead of her to his car parked around in back and had the motor started by the time she reached it. They raced down the long winding driveway to Telegraph Road.

They barely made it, had only just swung out onto the road when a car came toward them from around a curve, direction signal already flashing for a left-hand turn.

"Mrs. Baker!" Gretchen crouched down in the seat as she recognized the car. "She must have been the one who called. She knew something was wrong with Mrs. Engels talking about a bridge game and she's come over to find out what it is."

"Right," said Jay, watching in the rearview mirror. "She's going up the driveway now."

They had expected to have a full day's leeway before the cleaning woman was due again. Now, it seemed, they might have only minutes, perhaps, before Mrs. Baker took some sort of action. When she found the house locked up, the doorbell unanswered, Mrs. Engels's car out in front where Gretchen had left it, she might call the police immediately.

But Gretchen kept her head. She curbed Jay's instinct to drive fast when Telegraph Road widened out into a divided highway and they were headed for the Toledo Freeway. There was no need, she said, to take chances on being picked up for speeding.

"It's not as if Mrs. Baker could give the police a description of your car," she said. "There was no reason for her to notice it, she doesn't know it exists. Or that you exist, Jay."

"She might have noticed the Illinois plates."

"Even if she did, look at all the traffic we're in now. No one could pick us out."

No one did. But even when they got on the freeway and left Detroit safely behind, it took time for their sense of having narrowly averted disaster to fade. There was always, Gretchen brooded to herself as the miles fell away, the unexpected. It was an occupational hazard they had to accept. The phone was the greatest risk of all; essential to their projects, however, and therefore an unavoidable risk; she had given it much thought but could find no way around it.

Today it had almost led to disaster.

She voiced this thought aloud. "If Mrs. Baker had come two or three minutes earlier—"

"Then we'd have had to kill her too," Jay said flatly.

"Oh . . . Well, yes, I suppose so." Gretchen made a grimace. "But—a complication. You know how I like to plan things ahead down to the last detail. What happened with Mrs. Engels, that nothing, that cipher was bad enough as it was. The last person you'd expect to pull a trick like that on us."

Jay shrugged. "That's people for you." His eyes were on the road, his posture relaxed now, hands easy on the steering wheel.

Gretchen glanced at him, assessing his unworried attitude. Jay, on his own, wouldn't get away with robbing a piggy bank.

Florida was their ultimate destination but she had settled on a roundabout route taking the Ohio Turnpike east, not traveling too late that night. Tomorrow, she said, studying the map, they would start heading south from the Pennsylvania Turnpike but they would keep off the big roads just in case anyone, by an inconceivable chance, had noticed Jay's car with its Illinois plates in the vicinity of Mrs. Engels's.

Jay scoffed, as always, at her excessive caution but had to concede that they had all the time in the world to reach Florida.

They stopped for dinner at a service area on the Ohio Turnpike and at ten o'clock, approaching the Pennsylvania border, took an exit ramp to a motel.

Jay signed them in. Gretchen, still in the black wig and garb of Mrs. Engels's companion, kept out of sight in the car.

They had drinks in their room before going to bed.

Gretchen sat in front of the mirror, removing hairpins, shaking the wig loose to see how it would look if she had it cut short.

"You know, I just might do that when I don't need it for any more projects," she informed Jay over her shoulder. "How would you like me as a brunette, darling? Just for a change, I mean."

"Not in that particular wig," he retorted, "or the brown one that you won't get rid of."

This was familiar ground. "I've told you how much they cost, Jay. Why should I get rid of them when I'd just have to go out and buy new ones? You're the one who's being too cautious now."

"Maybe. But whatever they cost, it's nothing to the money they've brought in. Not from Mrs. Engels, though." A bleak note came into his voice. "She turned out to be a real lemon. The money and the jewelry too. Only two diamond rings, a few bracelets and brooches. Nothing like what we hoped for. And then making all that trouble for us at the end."

Gretchen was quick to defend herself since it had been her decision that Mrs. Engels was a good prospect. "Well, over thirteen thousand in cash plus whatever we get for her jewelry isn't too bad for three months' work," she pointed out.

"Got to do better next time, though," Jay said. "You're the one who keeps telling me we can't take the pitcher to the well too often and that we've got our retirement goal to meet."

"We'll make it," Gretchen spoke with assurance. "Five years, I said, and only fourteen months of them are gone. There'll be a big one next time or the time after that. Wait and see."

She turned back to the mirror to study the wig again. "I believe I will have it cut someday. Be fun to wear it now and then."

"Go right ahead," Jay said. "You make all the decisions anyway, don't you?"

Gretchen ignored the resentment in his voice. She took off the wig, combed it out and put it away in its case.

11

Late one afternoon the middle of August, Mrs. Mercer called wanting to know if she might come over and talk to them about something that had just come up. "If it wouldn't inconvenience you," she said.

"No, not at all," Gretchen replied. "Except that we're just back from the beach and starting to take showers. So in half an hour, perhaps?"

"That'll be fine."

Jay was already in the shower. When he came out Gretchen told him about the call.

"Wonder what she wants." He frowned as he toweled himself dry. "You don't think—?"

"Of course not. Anything like that, she wouldn't come near us herself. She'd call the police." Gretchen tossed the bra top of her bikini over a towel bar, took off the bottoms and turned on the water for her shower. "Must be some domestic problem," she added, raising her voice to be heard over it.

Mrs. Mercer was on her way somewhere else when she arrived soon after five-thirty, hair freshly done, black and white print cocktail dress, the diamond bracelet Jay never failed to notice glittering on her wrist.

"A cocktail party," she said when Gretchen complimented her on her appearance.

She got around a lot for a woman her age, thought Gretchen, who considered anyone in their sixties on the edge of the grave. And entertained a lot too. They had been avoiding guests on her terrace all summer.

"Can't we give you a head start?" Jay queried. "We're about to have a drink ourselves."

"Well, just a quick one. Scotch and water, please." Mrs. Mercer took the chair Gretchen indicated.

She hadn't seen much of her tenants these past several

Only Couples Need Apply 73

weeks; she had almost forgotten her uneasy feelings over them earlier in the summer. Now, while Jay was fixing the drinks, her thoughts didn't go beyond how clean-cut and wholesome they looked. It was too bad about the apartment. But blood was thicker than water . . .

She waited until they were settled with their drinks, Jay and Gretchen opposite her on the sofa, and then began, "I've been wondering how much longer you plan to keep the apartment. As I recall it, Mrs. Addison," her glance went to Gretchen, "you said when you took it that your plans were indefinite but you'd stay through the summer, at least."

"Yes, something like that," Gretchen agreed, her tone guarded, not sure yet what this was leading to. "Depending on how my husband got on with his book."

Jay fastened his attention on his drink. Had Mrs. Mercer found out what had really happened to her dog? No, she couldn't have. It was over a month ago now.

Her glance strayed to the typewriter table. The stack of manuscript seemed a slight showing for three months' work. But then, she knew too little about writing to make a judgment.

"How's your book coming, Mr. Addison?" she asked.

"Slowly," he replied as if reading her thought. "I'm not trying to hurry it."

He looked at her bracelet again, diamonds sparkling in a ray of sunlight as she twisted it absently. How much was it worth?

"The reason I ask," Mrs. Mercer continued, "is that I have a problem about my sister in Bedford, Massachusetts. Her husband died last fall and she sold the house in April this year—rather in too much of a hurry, I thought at the time—promising occupancy October 1."

"Oh," said Gretchen, realizing now the purpose of the visit.

"She bought a lot and had plans drawn for a smaller house but there have been all sorts of delays over it. She can't find anything else she wants so it seems she's more or less stranded . . ."

Mrs. Mercer, looking embarrassed, took a swallow of her drink and resumed, "She called me earlier today and asked about this apartment. She'd like to rent it, she said, for at least six months starting October 1. She would put her own furniture in storage and take her time buying or building another house. So I thought, if you people are planning to leave anyway at the end of the summer..." Her voice trailed off into silence.

"Yes, of course," Gretchen said coolly. "Naturally, your sister comes first. Why don't we say the middle of September, Mrs. Mercer? We took the apartment the middle of May and we've been paying our rent on that basis ever since."

"You're sure you don't mind?"

"Not at all." Gretchen glanced at Jay. "Do we, dear?"

"No indeed."

"Well then, thank you so much. I do appreciate your understanding my position." Mrs. Mercer gave them a relieved smile and stood up to leave. "You've been such fine tenants, I'll regret losing you."

Gretchen returned her smile politely. "We'll be sorry to leave," she said. "But there's still a month left and Jay has at least made a start on his book. He hopes he'll have it finished by spring."

"You must let me know when it's going to be published," Mrs. Mercer said. "I'll look forward to reading it."

Gretchen walked her to the door and closed it after her. When her footsteps receded on the stairs she said lightly, "Well, first time I've ever been evicted."

"Me too." Jay got to his feet and picked up their glasses. "Calls for another drink." On his way to the kitchen he added, "That diamond bracelet. Knock your eyes out, wouldn't it?"

"Forget it," Gretchen said. "You've had her jewelry on your mind since the day we arrived here."

But Jay couldn't. "Too bad we didn't come across her when we were getting ready to set up a project," he said as he started making their drinks. "Real haul, I'll bet."

"Sometimes, Jay, I can't even imagine what goes on in your head," Gretchen said sarcastically. "We'd never get anywhere with Mrs. Mercer. In the first place, she's not about to hire a companion and in the second place she'd never let anyone else handle her finances. So how would you go about getting hold of her jewelry—hit her over the head and rob her?"

"Maybe," he replied. "Maybe just that." He handed

Gretchen her drink and followed her back into the living room.

"You mean—at least I hope you do—that you might go about it that way if she were a perfect stranger who had no connection whatsoever with us."

Jay shrugged, said nothing.

"But if you're talking as if it were something you really might do before we leave, how would you plan to keep the police off your tail?" The sarcastic note in Gretchen's voice deepened. "After all, we've been around here all summer."

"I was just talking," Jay said with a resentful look.

"Well, it's more to the point to talk about what we'll do next. We're being evicted, we've got to begin making plans."

"Our next project?" His resentment faded at the prospect of action.

"I don't see why not. It's over four months since Florida, no sign of the police beating a path to our door."

"Texas," he said, lighting a cigarette. "Some of those oil millionaires we hear about must die sometime and leave rich widows who need a meek little companion to look after them."

"Houston, maybe. What if I get another wig? How would I look as a redhead?"

"Stunning," Jay said, reaching for her.

"I wouldn't do it, though," she murmured as his mouth sought hers. "Too conspicuous."

"That's right." He put out his cigarette, his lips moving slowly over her cheeks, eyelids, throat. "You're the meek little companion who never says boo."

"Mmm," Gretchen murmured as he gathered her up and carried her into the bedroom. "Mmm . . ."

Later, as they lay beside each other in the darkened room, she said, "I've never been to Texas."

"Oil millionaires' widows live there," he reminded her, half asleep.

She propped herself up on one elbow and brushed his face with her fingers. "Maybe I should try to marry one of the millionaires myself instead of hiring out to their widows," she said. Her tone was light but Jay turned his head to look at her. "Keeping me in luxury on the side?"

"Right. And presently divorcing the millionaire and living happily ever after on alimony. How about it? Maybe that's the big killing we should look for."

"Maybe," he said. "Or maybe we should turn it around and I should marry one of the widows instead."

They weren't serious talking like that, Gretchen told herself. Or was there a thread of seriousness, deep-buried somewhere, at least on her part, if not on Jay's?

They were nearly ready to go out to dinner when Mrs. Mercer drove in at eight o'clock. They heard the electric-eye door descending and then her brisk firm tread crossing the driveway to her back door.

"Old girl's real active for her age," Jay commented.

"All that golf helps keep her in good condition," said Gretchen.

Lights were on in Mrs. Mercer's bedroom when they went down to their car a few minutes later. She was getting out of her party clothes, putting away her diamond bracelet with the rest of her jewelry, Jay thought, glancing over at the house as he rolled up their garage door. Where did she keep it? Did she keep cash in the house too?

He doubted it. She seemed too sharp for that, very capable, as Gretchen had been so quick to point out, of taking care of her financial affairs.

Her jewelry, though, was his main interest. He'd got quite a hangup on jewelry, handling it every day in the store in Philadelphia. There was something about the really good pieces that got to him.

It bothered him sometimes having to part with them for maybe half their value or less after one of the projects.

He looked up at Mrs. Mercer's lighted windows again as he backed the car around and started down the driveway. She kept her jewelry in her room, probably, her back bedroom.

She had mentioned that she preferred to sleep in the back of the house away from street traffic that seemed to increase year by year, keeping pace with the growth of the town itself.

It was a preference that suited Jay's purpose. He intended to search her bedroom, her whole house, if necessary, to find the repository for her jewelry.

He wouldn't touch it, however, when he found it, except to look it over and make a quick appraisal of its total

Only Couples Need Apply

value. He hadn't needed Gretchen's reminder that they would be major suspects if anything was missing.

But why not make a future visit if it seemed worthwhile—a month or two, say, after they had given up the apartment and left town? Come back in a different car, keep a watch on the house until Mrs. Mercer went out for the evening, then make a fast haul of her jewelry and a fast getaway from Belmont.

It would be no problem to break the glass in the back door, force the lock to make it look like an outside job. It would keep the police from asking too many questions about former tenants who might have been able to get hold of her keys.

She must have the jewelry insured. A check from her insurance company would soon calm her down over her loss.

He would have to let Gretchen in on it when the time came, of course. She'd be furious at first over the chance he had taken getting the duplicate key made but she would calm down, too, once she realized what a foolproof plan he'd worked out for his project, not a big one, maybe, but the first one he could call his own.

That was all in the future, though. His immediate problem was lack of opportunity to get into the house, locate Mrs. Mercer's jewelry, look it over and make up his mind if it was worth the risk—no use kidding himself, there'd be a slight risk involved as Gretchen was sure to point out to him at great length—of going ahead with his plans.

Solving his immediate problem wasn't going to be easy, Jay reflected, making perfunctory replies to Gretchen's conversation as they drove to a restaurant on the other side of the lake. He didn't know just how he was going to manage it with only a month to go before they gave up the apartment. There was no telling when Gretchen would go to the laundromat at night again or if Mrs. Mercer would be safely out of the way when she did.

In fact, the only evening he'd been sure he had a clear field the goddamn dog had got underfoot and ruined it for him.

He couldn't count on another one like it. He'd have to figure out something else ...

Start taking a walk evenings they stayed home and get Gretchen used to it? She didn't care about walking herself, used the car just to go around the block. He could say he felt like stretching his legs and begin to keep an eye on Mrs. Mercer's comings and goings.

It was probably as good an approach as any, Jay thought, turning in at the restaurant.

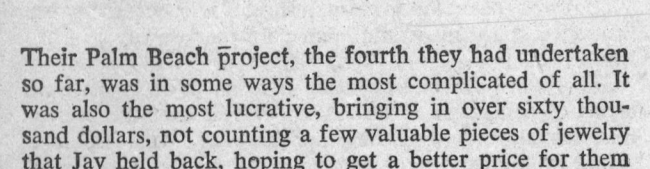

12

Their Palm Beach project, the fourth they had undertaken so far, was in some ways the most complicated of all. It was also the most lucrative, bringing in over sixty thousand dollars, not counting a few valuable pieces of jewelry that Jay held back, hoping to get a better price for them later.

They didn't reach Florida until after Labor Day, changing their plans after their first night on the road to spend a few days in Pittsburgh where they could be sure the Detroit *Free Press* would be available at some newsstand.

The second day they were there, Mrs. Engels's murder made the front page of the *Free Press* with the headline: WIDOW OF GENERAL MOTORS EXECUTIVE SLAIN. Birmingham police, the story said, had no definite leads yet but were seeking Miss Geraldine Cooper, twenty-eight, the dead woman's missing companion.

The fourth day the *Free Press* featured a police artist's sketch of Gretchen in her black wig and black-rimmed glasses that bore no resemblance to her out of disguise. And once again, as in the search for her after the Santa Barbara project, descriptions of Gretchen had her an inch or two shorter than her actual height and ten to fifteen pounds heavier than her actual weight.

Police speculation on the likelihood of a confederate in the robbery-murder came into the story although no one in Mrs. Engels's circle could offer evidence to support it, Geraldine Cooper never having been seen in the company of anyone, male or female, who might have been in collu-

Only Couples Need Apply

sion with her. There was nothing. Gretchen and Jay told each other in self-congratulation, that could ever connect them with it now.

"Least of all you," Gretchen said, putting the newspaper aside. "You're the invisible man."

"I wasn't in Santa Barbara."

"Almost, though. You didn't see any police sketches of you in the California papers, did you? I'm the one who's always out in the open. One of these days we'll do a switch. Watch the ads for an elderly man looking for a houseman or something."

"Sure," said Jay amiably. "No reason not to."

But there was, Gretchen knew. Jay couldn't cope with the role she played. He would get them both caught in no time.

Even though there was no way to get around this, a small kernel of resentment that the major risks would always be hers stayed in the back of Gretchen's mind and, as a corollary to it, the realization that if they had just been business partners, living separate lives between projects, she would be entitled to the larger share of the profits.

Such a thought, she knew, had never entered Jay's head.

Perhaps one day she would have to see that it did.

Not yet though. Not while the disappointing take from Mrs. Engels still rankled and had already led to the decision that they would start looking for a new project as soon as they were settled in Florida.

John and Gertrude Simmons were their new names. They used them when they bought traveler's checks and registered as Mr. and Mrs. John Simmons at their Pittsburgh motel.

Jay sold Mrs. Engels's few pieces of jewelry and got rid of his gun before they headed south.

They spent a few days at Sea Island, Georgia, on the way and discussed what part of Florida would suit them best.

Jay suggested the west coast. "Lots of old people. There must be plenty of good prospects."

But Gretchen shook her head. "Not as many as you think. Mostly pensions and social security types. The real money's on the east coast. Palm Beach or somewhere in that area. We'll look around."

It was off-season in Florida, reduced rates, plenty of vacancies to pick and choose from. The choice they made was an oceanfront luxury apartment a few miles south of Palm Beach. They might have been any moneyed young couple staying there on vacation—except that they discouraged friendly overtures from fellow residents—settling into a routine of swimming, lazing on the beach, dining and dancing at the better night spots, playing a little tennis.

Beneath this façade, Gretchen began preparing for their next project. She bought the usual assortment of unattractive clothes for it and wearing one of her new outfits, her brown wig and glasses, rented an efficiency apartment in West Palm Beach as Miss Gertrude Simmons. That was the name and address she used applying for a Florida driver's license.

Once this background was established she began to study help wanted ads in the Palm Beach *Post-Times* and the Miami *Herald*.

The first prospect wouldn't do at all. She had a son living nearby who dropped in every day or two.

The second, in Delray Beach, seemed made to order for a project—spinster with no inconvenient relatives and every sign of money. She hired Gretchen, Jay flying to Charleston, South Carolina, to attest to the excellent care Miss Simmons had given his late mother.

But two days before Gretchen was to move in, the spinster had a heart attack and was presently sent home with a nurse in attendance.

"Money and effort wasted," Jay complained.

"We can't win them all," Gretchen said, coming home from a visit to the spinster who had been apologetic over having to terminate a promised job before it had even begun. "Look"—she took a check out of her pocketbook—"two weeks' salary to make up for some of it. In case I'd missed another job in the meantime."

"She'll never know that her heart attack was the least of her troubles," said Jay.

"So we wait for something else to turn up," Gretchen said.

As it did only a week later through an ad in the Palm Beach *Post-Times*. Live-in companion, light housework

Only Couples Need Apply

weekends, driver's license, references, box number for replies.

"Lot of lonely old women in the world," Gretchen commented, getting out her plain good quality notepaper to reply to it.

She spent most of the next few days in her West Palm Beach efficiency waiting for a letter or a phone call. It was boring but at least, she consoled herself, she liked to read; particularly mysteries and real-life crime stories. That helped to pass the time.

Finally the call came, a wheezy asthmatic voice asking for Miss Gertrude Simmons, arranging an interview for the next day, Friday, October 15, at two o'clock.

Gretchen phoned Jay afterward. "Tomorrow afternoon at two o'clock," she said. "Mrs. Thomas Russell. Palm Beach."

They met an hour later, Gretchen in her rental car, Jay in the one they had bought.

"We'll just drive past for a look," Gretchen said, consulting the directions Mrs. Russell had given her.

The house was on A1A, a palatial white stucco residence, overlooking the ocean. A high brick wall painted white enclosed the extensive grounds of which little could be seen from the road.

"That's all to the good," said Jay.

"Let's hope the rest is," said Gretchen.

The first complication when she arrived for her interview the next afternoon was the uniformed Negro maid who admitted her and led the way to a spacious well-furnished living room. Full-time, not daily help. Did she sleep in too? There'd be ways around her, though, accusation of theft, maybe. How would her word stand up against Gretchen's, black against white? It would probably depend on how long she had worked for Mrs. Russell.

The second complication took the form of an alert-looking woman somewhere around forty who came forward to greet Gretchen. "How do you do, Miss Simmons," she said. "I'm Sarah Clayton. I came down from New York earlier this week to help my mother arrange for a companion."

"How do you do," said Gretchen.

"My mother, Mrs. Russell."

Mrs. Russell was a mountain of a woman, overflowing

the largest chair in the room. No more than in her early sixties, Gretchen thought, but so imprisoned in her flesh that she leaned forward with some difficulty to extend her hand.

"Appreciate your coming to see me, Miss Simmons," she said in the wheezy voice of her phone call.

"My pleasure, Mrs. Russell," Gretchen replied, flashing one of her empty bright smiles as she took the proffered hand.

"Do sit down, Miss Simmons."

Gretchen settled herself sedately in a chair nearby prepared to answer questions. She gave her usual background story of attending a junior college—this time it was a small private secretarial school in Los Angeles that had closed down for good soon after she arrived there last year—and went on to the elderly aunt she had taken care of during a long terminal illness and her employment after that as companion/secretary to a retired businesswoman in Atlanta who had died two months ago.

"That's the only job you've ever had, Miss Simmons?" Mrs. Clayton's tone expressed discontent with this one job reference.

Mrs. Russell, amiable looking in contrast to her daughter, said nothing.

"Yes, it is," replied Gretchen. "I was with her five years, you see."

"Oh, five years." She could read Mrs. Clayton's thought that she must have given satisfaction.

"Her son, Mr. Marshall Loman, travels a lot but he's in Atlanta right now settling Mrs. Loman's estate. I wrote to him about a job reference and he wrote back the other day that if I needed it within the next week or so, he could be reached at the Regency Hyatt starting tomorrow."

Jay would have to make a reservation there and fly to Atlanta tonight.

"Mr. Marshall Loman, Regency Hyatt." Mrs. Clayton made a note of it just as she had with the name and address of the junior college. Just let her try to track down its records, though. There had been a minor scandal connected with its closing that had got written up in the Los Angeles papers. Gretchen had clipped the stories on it and kept them in case of future need. Which, with someone like Mrs. Clayton, was now.

"I'm sure you understand, Miss Simmons, that I feel I should be very careful in helping my mother to select a companion."

"Of course."

"It worries me at times, Mother living here and I, her only child, living in New York."

"Oh, Sarah, don't fuss so," Mrs. Russell said in a sudden assertion of authority. "This will be the third winter since your father died and up to now I've been perfectly all right here by myself." She gave Gretchen an easygoing smile. "It's really my daughter's idea that I shouldn't be alone any more. Do you play bridge, my dear?"

"Well, party bridge. I'm not an expert."

"Neither am I. Or my friends. Sometimes we need a fourth."

Mrs. Atwood all over again, thought Gretchen.

"And you drive a car?" Mrs. Clayton, thin, restless, played with a chunky assortment of bracelets on her wrist.

"Yes, for several years. I just got a Florida license."

"Let me see . . . Why did you say you came to Florida if your home was in California?"

"I don't think it's been mentioned, Mrs. Clayton. But I used to live in Delaware with my aunt and I really prefer the east coast. I decided on Florida because I enjoyed coming here two or three times on vacation."

"I see."

Gretchen sensed that as in earlier projects, her drab appearance, unassuming but capable manner were making a favorable impression on Mrs. Clayton. She suspected, as question and answer continued, that Mrs. Clayton suffered some pangs of conscience over not having her mother live with her. This, after it became clear that Mrs. Russell now lived the year around in her Palm Beach home.

". . . Although we do insist, Miss Simmons, that Mother must spend a few weeks with us at our place on Long Island during the summer . . ."

But not next summer, it seemed, with the Claytons already making plans for a European trip that did not include Mother.

It also developed that while the Claytons would spend

Thanksgiving with Mrs. Russell, there wasn't much prospect that they would be able to visit her again all winter.

In other words, she was being shunted aside and once Mrs. Clayton found a suitable companion for her, would be shunted aside still more.

The situation looked more favorable to Gretchen at the end of the interview than at the beginning.

"You'll hear from us, Miss Simmons," Mrs. Clayton said, walking to the door with her.

"She'll check me out all she can," Gretchen reported to Jay driving him to the airport to take a plane to Atlanta. "But the mother liked me; no trouble pleasing her."

"I hope to hell this one works out," he said. "No fun sitting around a hotel in Atlanta, not knowing a soul."

But they both knew he soon would. There'd be bars, there'd be girls.

There always were, Gretchen thought acidly. The best she could hope for was that he'd keep his mouth shut. God, how he turned her off sometimes . . .

Mrs. Clayton called Gretchen the next week to tell her she was hired. "I must get back to New York myself tomorrow," she said, "but my mother hopes you'll be able to be with her this coming Monday. Will that suit you all right, Miss Simmons?"

"Oh yes. Let's say around ten o'clock Monday morning."

Lengthy instructions followed; about calling Mrs. Clayton in New York if any questions came up; about her mother's overeating; "Dr. Wells and I have both been trying to get her to diet but she won't listen to us . . ."; about trying to get her more interested in outside activities; "So bad for her to sit around the house so much playing bridge and watching television . . ."; and so forth. Gretchen stopped listening, saying yes to everything, including the salary already tentatively discussed.

No mention, though, she noticed, of not being able to get in touch with the defunct junior college in Los Angeles. Had Mrs. Clayton even tried to—or just been content, on Jay's recommendation, to dump her responsibilities on her mother's new companion?

The following Monday, beginning the last week of October, Gretchen was established in her room at Mrs. Russell's, a comfortable, well-furnished room, the furniture moved down from the Westchester house Mrs. Russell and her late husband had lived in until he retired and they moved to Palm Beach.

"Very nice," she told Mrs. Russell. "I'm sure everything will be just fine."

That same Monday Jay gave up their apartment and moved into another one in a larger complex that offered anonymity.

Gretchen eased her way into the household. She let a week go by before she asked Mrs. Russell to call her by her first name; and another week before she began taking charge of domestic affairs. But by the time Mrs. Clayton, her taciturn husband and two pre-teen children arrived for Thanksgiving, her role was clearly defined as Gertrude, dear, will you see about this, will you take care of that?

Mrs. Clayton observed, approved of her choice. When she left for the airport with her family the following Sunday she felt that her mother was in good hands and that all concern about her could be dismissed.

"I can't get used to all this rushing around nowadays," Mrs. Russell said plaintively, turning from the doorway where she had waved a last good-by. "Just think, Gertrude, how soon they'll be back in New York."

"With ice and snow to contend with while we're sitting under palm trees," Gretchen reminded her.

"True." Mrs. Russell, waddling back to her chair, brightened for a moment, then added with a sigh, "But it will be such a long time before I see them again. Sarah said last night I mustn't even count on their getting down for Easter next year," She paused. "Sometimes, Gertrude, I do feel cut off, you know."

"I know." Gretchen put her hand on her arm to guide her into her chair. "But you mustn't let yourself dwell on it, Mrs. Russell. Perhaps we should do something tonight to take your mind off it. Is there a movie you'd like to see or anything like that?"

"Well, no, not a movie, but"—Mrs. Russell brightened again—"why don't we go out to dinner? Somewhere special."

Dinner. She would eat herself into her grave if Gretchen and Jay didn't hurry the process.

"Whatever you say," Gretchen replied.

The maid's name was Betty Mae Burnett. She lived in

some back street, tucked out of sight of the rich folk, to which she retreated at the end of her working day. Betty Mae, thirtyish, uncommunicative, had only been with Mrs. Russell a little over two years. There was no particular rapport Gretchen soon discovered, between mistress and maid. Betty Mae was dropped off at the house every morning by her brother-in-law and picked up every evening by her husband. Mrs. Russell's easygoing attitude toward her made no impression. Betty Mae kept in her place.

It would be no great problem to discredit her, Gretchen told Jay on one of their days off. A few questions, for instance, about a sapphire ring she sometimes wore and sometimes left in her room. Have you seen it, Betty Mae? I'm sure I left it in the box on my bureau. You remember it, Mrs. Russell, the one the salesgirl admired the other day in that boutique on Worth Avenue?

So the seed would be planted in Mrs. Russell's mind, the first small doubt of Betty Mae's honesty. To be built up gradually, not to reach a climax, Gretchen said, until they were nearly ready to act. Otherwise, Mrs. Russell would just hire someone else.

The gardener? He only came Mondays and Thursdays. Brought his own lunch, had little contact with Mrs. Russell except to be paid.

In her role of companion, Gretchen built up Mrs. Russell's dependence on her, always there when needed, pampering her, running errands, taking on more and more responsibility, winning the liking of Mrs. Russell's friends, most of them spinsters or elderly widows like herself.

"Not any men to worry about," Gretchen told Jay. "Just a few decrepit old husbands or brothers or something like that. It's Mrs. Clayton's calls that bother me. There's no regular pattern to them. What would we do if she insisted on speaking to her mother just when we were in the middle of the project?"

They were at the beach that day, Gretchen's day off. It was the only chance she ever had to go swimming. Mrs. Russell had urged her to at first but Gretchen, thickset in her layers of clothing, couldn't display herself, slender and trim in a swim suit. She had to say she was afraid of the water.

Jay went in every day and developed a magnificent tan

Only Couples Need Apply

while Gretchen watched hers fade away except on her face and arms which she was careful to keep tanned to look right with her wig.

Gretchen's pampering of Mrs. Russell, all the little extra touches she provided for her comfort, encouraged the lethargy Mrs. Russell's great weight induced.

It didn't take long to get her out of the habit of going to the bank with Gretchen. "Can't I just run over by myself, Mrs. Russell? ... Deposit the dividend checks? Glad to ... One hundred in cash? Certainly, Mrs. Russell ..."

Gretchen became a familiar figure, her status accepted without question at Mrs. Russell's bank.

And soon thereafter at her broker's, too, where she had an active account, following the stock market closely, placing regular orders to buy or sell. She had got interested in it, she told Gretchen, through her late husband who had been a member of a Wall Street investment firm right up until his retirement.

Early in February, Mrs. Russell, wanting a stock certificate that was in her safe deposit box, decided it was too much trouble to keep going back and forth to the box herself.

"Run over to the bank, Gertrude, and get me one of their forms or cards or whatever I have to sign to give you access to it," she said. "Have them call me if there's any other red tape we have to go through. The certificate is overdue at my broker's now. I'd like you to deliver it to him yourself later today."

"Yes, Mrs. Russell. As soon as I'm able to get it."

A week later Mrs. Russell had an argument over the phone with her broker that led Gretchen to thoughts of giving a more ambitious twist to the project.

The argument grew out of a phone call from Mrs. Russell's son-in-law in New York urging her to buy into a new electronics company on Long Island. He had private information that the company would announce the signing of a big government contract before the week was out. Get in now, get in fast, he said, before the news broke.

Mrs. Russell looked at her bank balance, pored over the list of her stock holdings deciding what she would sell. She sent Gretchen to the bank to get the certificates out of her safe deposit box and take them to her broker.

Then Mrs. Russell called him. She wanted the stock sold immediately, she said, and her money the next day.

Impossible, said the broker and talked at great length about Securities and Exchange Commission rules.

Nothing was impossible, said Mrs. Russell.

Voices sharpened on both sides. At last, however, as she overruled all his protests, he caved in and agreed that Miss Simmons could pick up the check the next morning.

"Now that she's got away with it once, there's no reason she shouldn't get away with it again," Gretchen said reporting the incident to Jay. "It just means keeping her alive overnight in case any problem came up with her broker the next day. Take his check back to her, make her endorse it and then call her bank saying she wants the money in cash."

"Jesus, it's going to take plenty of nerve," Jay said.

Gretchen gave him a level look. "I've got it," she said.

13

Toward the middle of March, Mrs. Clayton called to tell her mother it was now definite that they wouldn't be down over Easter. Instead, her husband felt, they should spend Easter week with his brother in Jamaica.

As a sop to her mother's disappointment Mrs. Clayton added that perhaps a little later on when the children were back in school she might be able to fly down for two or three days herself. "Why don't you and Miss Simmons make your own plans for Easter," she suggested. "Take a cruise or something."

"Maybe we will," said Mrs. Russell, although they both knew she wouldn't bestir herself that much.

Gretchen knew it too.

"Easter week," she told Jay. "The Claytons safely out of the way, Mrs. Russell's annuity check due plus some dividend checks that should be coming in."

Only Couples Need Apply

"There's still the maid."

"I'm already working on that, dropping little seeds of suspicion in the old girl's mind. I'll have Betty Mae fired within the next couple of weeks. Something planted in her pocketbook as the final touch. Then I'll offer to take care of things myself or just get a cleaning woman in until after Easter when people will be going back north and there'll be a good selection of maids to choose from."

Gretchen paused with a faint cold smile. "Think how grateful Mrs. Russell will be. And how cut off from everyone. Not even her best friend, Mrs. Benson, around. She'll be in New Orleans visiting her son and daughter-in-law."

Gretchen paused again. "Let's make it Tuesday of Easter week. The gardener comes Monday."

By this time, working on their fourth project, they were used to their victims' first shocked moments of disbelief, jaws that flew open, frozen expressions, dawning realization that it wasn't some sort of monstrous joke. Then individual reactions set in. Mr. Sherman's face had kept its frozen look right up until she left the house, Gretchen remembered. Mrs. Atwood had turned numb. Mrs. Engels kept making squeaky sounds.

Mrs. Russell began to sweat, globules of moisture running down her face, collecting on her three chins. She licked it from the corners of her mouth with a flicking tongue. The underarms of her dress showed a spreading stain.

It was all that gross blubber ballooning out from her bones, Gretchen thought, as she gasped, "Gertrude—this man—what—?" She gestured limply toward Jay who smiled cheerfully with his gun pointed at her.

"Gertrude—" Mrs. Russell struggled to heave her bulk out of the chair.

"Stay where you are, Mrs. Russell. That's right—" As Jay took a step forward she sank back. "Just don't make a fuss and everything will be all right." Gretchen unplugged the phone on the table beside her and moved it away out of reach. "Just do as you're told . . ."

It was a little before ten on a sunny morning that would turn hot by noon.

"This is what I want you to do, Mrs. Russell," Gretchen said. "Call your broker and tell him you're sending me over with your three hundred shares of Emerson Electric and that you want him to sell it immediately and give you the check tomorrow. Like the other time, remember, when you made him pay you right away?"

"But—"

"It's not all that much, not to you. He won't refuse, as he might if it were more."

"I—I wouldn't even be able to speak—" Mrs. Russell's voice had a choked wheezy sound.

"I'll get you one of your pills and a glass of water," Gretchen said.

She left the room and came back with pills and a glass of water.

"There," she said, as Mrs. Russell took one and a few swallows from the glass.

After giving her a few moments to quiet down Gretchen said, "Don't try anything on the phone, Mrs. Russell. If you do, we'll have to kill you and that's the last thing we want to do. We just want some money."

Her candid look reinforced her words. Mrs. Russell, reassured, relaxed a little. There was no threat to her life—and what was money she would never miss compared to that?—as long as she did what she was told.

Gretchen waited another few moments to let her quiet down still more. Then she plugged the phone back in, dialed the broker's number and handed the receiver to her.

The broker said no, at first, as he had before, which put Mrs. Russell, in a grotesque sort of way, briefly on their side. Was he going to refuse her a simple favor after all the business she'd given him? she asked almost indignantly.

Finally, on the basis that it would never happen again, the broker agreed.

"Very good," Gretchen said when she hung up. "Would you like another drink of water before you call the bank?"

Mrs. Russell would. Gretchen brought it, then produced for her signature the annuity check that had come yesterday and a personal check for six thousand that left little in Mrs. Russell's account. When she had signed a form authorizing withdrawal of seven thousand from savings Gretchen said, "Your safe deposit key. Then call your bank and tell them you want all the money in cash."

It went without a hitch. The bank, the return to the house for Mrs. Russell's signature on the stock certificates, the delivery of them to the broker.

Only Couples Need Apply 91

Gretchen didn't get back to the house from her second trip until two o'clock. She made sandwiches and coffee, reminding Jay, who wore gloves, to be careful about what he touched when he took them off to eat.

Mrs. Russell found solace in having Gretchen wait on her as if nothing had changed. She was able to eat.

The phone rang. A flicker of hope showed on her face as Gretchen answered it, died when Gretchen said, "Oh, I'm sorry, Miss Stanley, but we're just leaving and Mrs. Russell is already out in the car . . . No, we won't be back until late tonight."

"Now the key to your jewelry drawer, Mrs. Russell."

It was in the closet in the toe of an evening slipper.

"Silly place," Gretchen said. "Just a matter of time for anyone to find it."

"Oh, you dreadful, wicked—" Mrs. Russell choked with fury.

She was regaining spirit now that fear had waned. She had to do what these awful people said but as long as she didn't cross them they wouldn't harm her. Afterward though, she would get the police after them as fast as she could! She studied Jay's face—how could such a clean-cut-looking young man be such a scoundrel?—fixing it in her memory, taking consolation from the thought of how well she would be able to describe him to the police. Gertrude, too, horrible, deceitful creature that she was.

The rest of the day dragged itself out. After she had served TV dinners Gretchen said to Jay, "This is a bit much. Let's get Mrs. Russell settled for the night."

"Good idea." Jay smiled his cheerful smile at their victim. "Off to bed, old lady."

Gretchen accompanied her into her downstairs bedroom, unplugged her phone and handed it to Jay who stood outside the room while Mrs. Russell undressed and protested once again over having to leave the bathroom door open while she used it.

"There is the window," Gretchen said. "Too small for you to squeeze all your fat through but still a window."

Mrs. Russell said nothing. She wouldn't speak to either of them again, she decided, until it was all over. She would save everything she had to say for the police.

But she broke this silent promise to herself when Jay

appeared with a length of nylon rope right after she got into bed.

"You're not going to tie me up!"

"We must, old lady, we must." The same cheerful smile, the same brisk tone.

"But I won't sleep a wink. I have to be able to turn over—"

"No problem." Gretchen left and came back with two sleeping pills while Jay was tying her expertly to the bed.

Mrs. Russell tried to resist. But he propped her head up and held her nose until she opened her mouth and swallowed them.

They left her weeping and exclaiming over what terrible people they were but her laments soon petered out. The pills were potent. She was snoring when Gretchen looked in on her a little later.

They killed her the next afternoon. They hadn't let her out of her room at all that day, Gretchen untying her just long enough to use the bathroom and eat her breakfast and once again to endorse the check from the broker.

When Gretchen returned from cashing it she was ready to begin on her final chore of wiping off fingerprints.

She had packed the night before and cleaned her room thoroughly to remove all traces of her presence there.

While Jay put her luggage and their strongbox in the car she talked to Mrs. Russell. They would have to leave her tied up like this for a few hours, she said, but once they were safely away they would phone the police to come and free her.

Mrs. Russell listened hopefully, not noticing how remote Gretchen's eyes were. These creatures would soon be out of her house; she might be able to free herself before they ever called the police.

Jay came into the room, the gun behind his back until the last moment when he pressed it against her head and fired.

She died instantly. Once they were sure of that they left the room without a backward glance.

Jay had driven his car into an empty stall in the garage.

"Just like Santa Barbara," Gretchen said as she got into it.

"That was a year ago and three thousand miles away."

"Even so . . ." Gretchen was pensive as he followed

signs from A1A to I-95 North. "The police call it MO, modus operandi. They catch people that way."

"But that's when they operate in the same area. We don't. Santa Barbara, Detroit, Palm Beach. Look how far apart they are."

"Almost sort of a triangle."

"Maybe we pick Texas next time and make it a quadrangle." Jay gave her a cocky grin. "How much cash from this one?"

"Close to fifty thousand."

"And another fifteen to twenty thousand for the jewelry. Not bad." It was after midnight when they stopped at a motel in South Carolina. No one saw Gretchen go into their room in her Gertrude Simmons guise or come out the next morning as herself.

They stopped at various banks in North Carolina on their way north to buy traveler's checks as John and Greta Loomis. News broadcasts on the car radio said nothing about a murdered woman at Palm Beach. They spent the night at a motel in Maryland and signed in the next day at the St. Regis in New York as Mr. and Mrs. John Loomis, Scranton, Pennsylvania. There was still nothing in the news about Mrs. Russell.

"We're home free," Jay exulted at dinner that night. "Even when they find her, who'd connect you with her companion?"

"Nobody," said Gretchen, sharing his confidence.

"She may not even be found until her daughter gets back from Jamaica next week."

"This Sunday," said Gretchen. "Then it should be a day or two after that."

But Mrs. Russell's murder made the news Sunday night. Her daughter arrived back in New York Saturday and getting no reply to repeated phone calls, contacted various friends of her mother's who said they hadn't been able to reach her themselves for the past several days. Mrs. Clayton then called the Palm Beach police who forced entry into the house and found the body. Miss Gertrude Simmons, the dead woman's companion for the past several months, was being sought for questioning.

The last item in the report was new to Gretchen and Jay.

"Mrs. Russell," said the announcer, "was the widow of

the late Harold Russell, senior member of the investment firm of Russell, Christman and Price, who in 1955 was indicted by a grand jury in an alleged stock swindle involving his firm. The charges were later dropped."

"No wonder she knew how to handle that broker of hers," Gretchen said.

The next morning Mrs. Russell's murder received front page coverage in the Miami *Herald*. Her companion, Gertrude Simmons, complete with description of brown hair and eyeglasses, the wrong height and weight, was prominently featured. Betty Mae Burnett, recently employed as a maid by Mrs. Russell, was being questioned by Palm Beach police.

Another day and the dead woman's bank and luckless stockbroker came into the picture. Also mentioned was the assumption that Gertrude Simmons might have had a confederate working with her although no trace of such a person had been uncovered.

Still another day and Gretchen once again saw a police artist's sketch of herself in a newspaper.

After that, as the days passed without new leads, the story dwindled and died.

Presently Jay felt it was safe to begin disposing of Mrs. Russell's jewelry a piece at a time, until most of it was sold.

Gretchen picked Addison for their new name and said that they could use their real first names when they cashed some of their traveler's checks and bought new ones. There was no reason they shouldn't, she said, since they were taking the summer off.

The second week of May they left New York with tentative plans for spending the summer in Maine.

They left after lunch. Late that afternoon Gretchen noticed the Belmont signs on I-84.

14

The opportunity Jay hadn't dared count on came his way one night only a week after he began establishing a pattern of evening walks. It came through Gretchen's sudden decision right after dinner to do the laundry that night instead of letting it go until tomorrow.

There was quite a lot of it, Jay noticed, carrying it down to the car. It would take Gretchen, so super-clean about everything, at least a couple of hours to get it done.

Not that it mattered unless Mrs. Mercer went out too. No sign of it yet. Ten of eight and her car was still there in the garage.

But just as Gretchen drove off Mrs. Mercer came out her back door.

Jay could scarcely believe his own luck. There she was, dressed to the nines, obviously going somewhere for the evening.

"Hi, Mrs. Mercer," he greeted her as she approached. "You off partying tonight?"

"Yes," she replied. "A housewarming party for some old friends who lived here years ago. He's retired now and they've moved back and bought a house."

"Well, have a good time." Jay opened the upstairs door. "Think I'll take a walk a little later myself. Gretchen's just left for the laundromat."

They said good night. He went upstairs and watched from the living-room window until Mrs. Mercer's car vanished from his sight.

Perfect setup, he thought. Light already fading, no damn dog to screw things up this time, Gretchen gone for at least two hours, Mrs. Mercer for the whole evening.

Take his time, though, getting the duplicate key and a flashlight; allow a few more minutes for it to get a little darker.

He paused in the doorway when he went downstairs. Cars passing on the street, headlights on now. The nearest houses on either side a hundred feet away with trees and shrubbery blocking their view of Mrs. Mercer's.

Jay moved quietly toward the back door, a shadow in the twilight. Mrs. Mercer had left the outside light on as usual, but there was no one to see him slip through the pool of brightness it cast and gain the shelter of the vine-covered back porch.

The next moment he was inside the house, the door closed and locked after him.

A night light burned in the kitchen but the shades were drawn.

He stood and listened. Nothing to hear, no one else in the house, the front hall too dark for him to see the stairway leading up to his goal, Mrs. Mercer's back bedroom.

His flashlight, shaded by his hand, pointed the way to it. The stairs were carpeted. An occasional creak was all that betrayed his footsteps as he climbed them. A front window in the upstairs hall reminded him to shade the flashlight still more as he swept it back and forth to get his bearings.

The first door to his left led into a bathroom; the second stood open on a bedroom, Mrs. Mercer's room, quickly identified. Shades drawn to the sills and curtains partly drawn gave him a sense of safety as he flashed his light around.

Heavy Victorian furniture, sleigh bed, nightstand beside it, highboy, straight chairs, cushioned rocker and, on an inner wall, a bureau with a heavy old mirror above it. Jay paid no attention to the gift-wrapped package on it, among the toilet articles. Or to a square table covered with a fringed cloth that touched the floor standing near it in a corner.

His attention turned to the jewelry box on the bureau. Nothing but costume jewelry in it though. It wasn't even locked.

A wall safe behind one of the pictures? No.

He turned back to the bureau and went through the drawers one by one, careful not to disturb anything in his search for Mrs. Mercer's jewelry.

He found none of it. But as he stepped away from the bureau debating whether to search the closet or the high-

Only Couples Need Apply

boy next, he hit his ankle against a sharp edge of the table in the corner.

A sharp edge that close to the floor? Jay rubbed his ankle, straightened up and eyed the table. All that stood on it was the framed photograph of an older man, probably Mrs. Mercer's husband.

Jay set it on the bureau, lifted the fringed cloth and said on a note of satisfaction, "Well, what d'you know," as he saw the safe underneath.

It was very old. Maybe a hundred years old, he thought; so old that it didn't even have a combination lock, just a keyhole that would take a fairly large key, nothing like the ones on Mrs. Mercer's key ring, certainly not the kind she'd be apt to carry around with her.

Where would she keep it? Somewhere handy. It wasn't in the bureau. Try the highboy.

Mrs. Mercer had arranged to pick up a friend, Mrs. Parker, on her way to the housewarming. Mrs. Parker wasn't quite ready when she arrived but had left the screen door unlocked and called down from upstairs, "That you, Anna? Come on in. I'll only be a minute."

"No hurry, I'm a little early," Mrs. Mercer called back, going into the living room where she turned on a light and made herself comfortable with the evening paper, remembering that she hadn't read the bridge hand that night.

The phone rang. She heard Mrs. Parker overhead answering it on her bedroom extension. Her voice floated down the stairs, not what she said but the tones, changing from surprise to question to resignation.

Mrs. Mercer, studying the bridge hand, paid no attention. If she had been sitting South like the expert she would never in the world have dropped her king on East's ace—how could they be so clever and foresighted?—and so wouldn't have made the four heart bid. Not many people would ...

Mrs. Parker interrupted her musings running downstairs and halting in the doorway with a gift-wrapped package in her hand.

"That was Pete who just called—collect, of course—from the bus station in Putnam," she announced.

"But I thought he wasn't due back from camp for two or three days yet," said Mrs. Mercer.

"So did I," her friend replied. "But he's back, sitting in the bus station loaded down with luggage and I'll have to go get him. So you'd better go on to the party without me, Anna. I'll be very late if I ever make it at all. Offer my apologies and take my gift along, will you, in case I don't?"

She came into the room and handed the package to Mrs. Mercer who stood up exclaiming, "Good heavens, I forgot my own. Left it upstairs in my room somewhere. I'll have to go back and get it."

She hurried off, pausing at the door to say over her shoulder, "Give Pete my love and tell him I hope he had a nice summer."

"I will. All I hope is that he hasn't grown a beard," said Pete's mother.

Mrs. Mercer laughed. "Well, if he has, hope for a luxuriant one. Anything but a goatee."

It was only a few blocks back to her house. She parked near the front door. Quicker to go in that way and straight upstairs ...

Jay hunted through the highboy for the key to the safe, through boxes of shirt studs, cuff links, tie clasps, Masonic, signet, college rings, all presumably belonging to Mrs. Mercer's late husband—for God's sake, why didn't the woman get rid of the stuff?—and on through an overflow of her personal effects in other drawers.

If it had been a front bedroom he would have heard her car stop outside or her footsteps on the porch or her key opening the door.

As it was, in the back of the house, absorbed in his search of the highboy, Jay was completely unaware of Mrs. Mercer's return until he heard the front door close after her and light poured into the room as she pressed the hall switches upstairs and down.

"Oh Jesus," he said. He closed the bottom drawer as silently as he could and sprang to his feet as she started upstairs. His eyes darted this way and that in search of a hiding place and settled on the closet. It would have to be that, there was nowhere else he could hide.

Jay crossed the room to it in quick noiseless strides, stopping on the way to drop the cloth back down over the safe, barely closing the closet door behind him when the

Only Couples Need Apply

click of a switch and light shining in around the door frame told him that Mrs. Mercer had entered the room.

"Now where did I leave it?" she murmured to herself. "Oh"—her glance settled on the bureau—"there it is."

She walked over to the bureau, picked up the package, turned to leave, turned back slowly and set the package down. Edward's picture . . . Who had moved it?

She stood like a statue looking around her, eyes sharp, all her senses alert for other signs of the intruder.

Jay couldn't understand the complete silence in the room. What was Mrs. Mercer doing—just standing there? What had brought her back so soon, anyway, when she was supposed to be at a party? He edged deeper into the closet seeking better concealment behind her clothes.

For all his care, a wire hanger rattled slightly as he brushed against it.

He froze where he stood, hoping against hope that it hadn't been heard through the door.

But it had, directing Mrs. Mercer's attention to the closet, releasing her from immobility into action.

Her gun, her Smith & Wesson .32 . . . She moved quickly to the nightstand, got it out of the drawer.

"All right," she said, trying to keep her voice firm and clear. "Come out of the closet with your hands up. I've got a gun and I know how to use it."

A gun. Holy Christ, Jay said to himself, faced with total disaster. A gun.

Was she bluffing? No. A woman living alone in a big house with a lot of valuables . . .

It was like a nightmare, his kaleidoscopic review of his own folly, of what Gretchen would say or do, of the police brought into it, the searchlight of investigation turned on them both.

Mrs. Mercer seemed to know what he was thinking. "Come out this minute or I'll call the police," she said. "There's a phone right here by my bed."

It wasn't the one she wanted to use. She felt trapped up here on the second floor where the thief, whoever was in the closet, might try to rush her. The wall phone in the kitchen with the shoulder rest that left both her hands free would be better.

Police. God, he had to stop her somehow. He flung the

door open and stepped out, hands in the air, the flashlight in one of them.

"Mr. Addison!" Shock rang in her voice.

"Sorry I frightened you, Mrs. Mercer." He tried to smile, his gaze fastened on the gun. He lowered his arms to his sides. "I knew you were out and I thought I saw a light up here when I started to take a walk. The back door was unlocked—"

"Indeed not. I'm very careful about that. I checked it as I left. So suppose you tell me how you got into the house and what you're doing in my bedroom. Tell me downstairs, not up here."

Mrs. Mercer, keeping the gun aimed at Jay, moved back against the wall putting the length of the room between them. She gestured toward the door with her free hand. "Go ahead of me down the stairs. Don't make any false moves, either, or I'll shoot."

Not a chance of jumping her while she kept this much distance between them. Throw his flashlight at her from the doorway?

She anticipated his thought. "Leave your flashlight on the bureau."

He put it down, one prospect gone. What about the stairs, though? Could he whirl around and grab her, trip her up or something?

But at the head of the stairway she said, "Go down sidewise, Mr. Addison, with both hands on the banister in plain sight.

That removed any chance of action on the stairs, he sidling down them as directed, she careful to keep four or five steps behind.

A bullet could bridge that gap faster than he could.

At the foot of the stairs she said, "Straight down the hall now into the kitchen."

He turned and looked up at her. "Will you just let me go then, Mrs. Mercer?" he pleaded. "Just walk out the back door and we'll both forget this whole crazy thing ever happened? If you'll let me, I promise you Gretchen and I will move out first thing tomorrow, tonight if you insist, leave Belmont and never come back."

"Straight down the hall to the kitchen." Her tone was inexorable.

"Over by the refrigerator," she said, reaching for the

Only Couples Need Apply

wall switch just inside the kitchen door. The bright ceiling light came on, banishing the dimness of the night light.

They looked at each other, Mrs. Mercer's face grim, Jay's white under his tan.

"Stand back against the refrigerator door, Mr. Addison and tell me how you got into my house."

"Like I told you before. I thought I saw a light, the door was unlocked—"

"Don't bother repeating that lie," she interrupted. "Take a look at the catch in the middle of the knob. It's straight across. That means the door is still locked. So how did you get in, Mr. Addison? The truth this time."

"I locked it after me."

Mrs. Mercer's grim look deepened. "If you won't tell me the truth I'll call the police this minute." Her gesture indicated the wall phone a few steps away.

"My God, Mrs. Mercer, don't do that! It would ruin me. Gretchen would leave me—it's not as if I took anything, did any harm—I was just curious about your house, taking a look around—" Jay was almost babbling in his desperation.

"In that case, you won't object to turning out your pockets. Walk over to the table and put down everything in them."

Jesus, he thought, her key. It was in the same pocket as his wallet without which he never left the house. But he had no choice. He had to stall for time, watch for his moment.

He was wearing the blue-and-green-striped Pierre Cardin shirt he had bought early in the summer. He turned the breast pocket inside out. It was empty.

"Your pants pockets."

A penknife, change, a parking lot stub came out. He unbuttoned the back pocket where he kept his wallet, palming the key as he laid the wallet on the table. He had a clean folded handkerchief in the other back pocket. He slipped the key inside the folds and laid the handkerchief down flat beside the wallet.

"All right," said Mrs. Mercer as he turned the last pocket out. "Go back and stand against the refrigerator."

"Can I pick up my things first?"

"No. I want a closer look at them."

When he had taken up his former position she went

over to the table, the gun in one hand, the other free to handle his belongings.

The handkerchief was nearest her. Just a folded handkerchief, no reason for her to touch it ... Jay held his breath.

But Mrs. Mercer picked it up and the key, shiny new, obviously a duplicate key, dropped out onto the table.

She gave him an appalled look and said, "So that's it. That's how you got into my house. You got hold of mine somehow and had one made. What are you, Mr. Addison, a professional thief—and your wife too?"

"Mrs. Mercer—"

"You were trying to get into my safe when I interrupted you!"

"No, no, Mrs. Mercer, you've got it all wrong. I'm not a professional thief—you can see I haven't taken one thing—and Gretchen isn't involved in this at all. I just happened to have a chance—" Jay broke off as Mrs. Mercer headed for the phone. "What are you going to do?"

"Call the police."

"What!" Outrage, desperation came together in the cry. "You can't do that to me. You've no right—"

Mrs. Mercer stood against the wall, gun steady in one hand, the other reaching for the telephone receiver. But then came the moment when her gaze had to shift from Jay long enough to read the emergency police number on the list beside the phone.

Jay was waiting for it. He hurled himself across the room at her with murderous intent. He made it over half the way before Mrs. Mercer shot him. The bullet hit him in the chest. He staggered back and crashed down on the floor.

15

Mrs. Mercer stood paralyzed with horror for an interval—a few seconds, a minute, two or three?—staring helplessly at Jay.

He lay on his back, a red stain spreading across the front of his shirt. His legs jerked spasmodically. His mouth opened. He made an odd little sound as if trying to speak but all that came of it was a bubble of blood and then a sigh.

He was dead when Mrs. Mercer at last was able to move and knelt beside him.

She couldn't believe it at first, lifting his head gingerly, looking into his blank eyes.

"Dear God," she gasped, "Oh, dear God . . ."

She got to her feet, walked shakily into the sitting room and collapsed onto a chair.

What was she going to do?

As fresh, as green as if it were only yesterday the memory of what had happened five years ago came back to overwhelm her . . .

It was a summer night that time, too, but June, not late August, her husband only a few months dead, she not sleeping well, feeling very much alone, listening to the creakings and settlings of the old house at night, sometimes more nervous over them than she would admit to anyone, least of all herself, but sitting up in bed to listen, even getting up sometimes to try to trace them to their source. One night she felt so certain there was someone prowling around downstairs that she got her husband's revolver out of the nightstand and searched the whole house before she was satisfied that it was just her overwrought nerves playing tricks on her.

Until that night in June . . .

She had gone to bed early and for once, tired out after

a busy day, straight to sleep. She woke up around midnight, brought bolt upright in bed by a sound from downstairs, not the usual creakings, but a tinkling sound like glass breaking.

By the time she was on her feet, throwing on a robe, feeling for the gun in the drawer, there were other faint sounds and as she crept downstairs, the glint of a shaded flashlight in the dining room, the clink of silver.

Everything seemed to happen all at once after that, she turning on the light, pointing the gun at the man running for the back door, crying out, "Stop or I'll shoot," the man not stopping, rushing into the semidarkness of the kitchen, she not really meaning to shoot him, not really taking aim, just firing to halt him in his tracks, the gun making a loud explosion of sound, the man dropping in a heap on the floor, a bag of silver clattering to the floor beside him.

Only he wasn't a man at all. He was the high school boy from the other side of town who mowed her lawn. A quiet boy never saying much but never failing to come the day he was suppposed to.

He lay dead by her back door, her silverware around him and the broken pane of glass that showed how he'd got in—right after that she'd had a bolt put on the bottom of the door but there'd been none that night to keep him out and so he lay dead of a chance hit never meant to take his life.

His name was Hank Morrison. He had turned sixteen only the week before she killed him. He came from a family of eight children and had never been in trouble with the police.

There was a coroner's inquest, a verdict of justifiable homicide, no blame, no penalty attached to her but nothing could change the fact that Hank Morrison was dead a week after his sixteenth birthday.

She had paid for his funeral, given his weeping mother money toward starting his older brother in college.

She had thought she would never get over it. Friends were kind, the police considerate, but she had thought she would never get over it.

She had, of course, in time. So much so that a year ago last fall when there was a rash of burglaries in her neighborhood and a prowler was sighted in her yard she bought

Only Couples Need Apply

the Smith & Wesson to replace her husband's gun, got rid of after she had killed Hank Morrison.

She bought it out of town and never mentioned it to anyone. Guns were, in any event, a subject those close to her were careful not to discuss in her presence.

But now there was another body on her kitchen floor. It didn't seem possible that it could happen twice to her, but it had. She would have to go through the whole terrible business again, all the worse because it would revive the story of Hank Morrison's death.

Justifiable homicide as before, only much more justified with Jay Addison than with poor young Hank. Even so, she would never live it down, not the second time around.

She couldn't face it, the publicity, the shame, the disgrace.

She wouldn't, she just wouldn't, that was all.

She got to her feet, went to the dining room and drank a small glass of brandy. It steadied her a little. She began to collect herself and look for a way out.

A plan. Thoughts scuttled around in her head but first the party—

She looked at her watch. Only twenty minutes, no more than that, had passed since her return home.

She went upstairs to call her hostess and explain that something had come up that would make her late. Her voice sounded normal. She even mentioned Janet Parker's unexpected trip to Putnam that might keep her from getting to the party at all.

Then, collecting an armful of sheets and the forgotten gift that had brought death to Jay, Mrs. Mercer hurried downstairs.

Her first move was to drive her car close to the back door. She let herself into the house that way and walked past Jay's body with averted gaze to the utility room off the kitchen for an old plastic raincoat that hung there.

She put it on, buttoned it up to cover her dress completely and went to get the sheets left in the hall.

There could be no averting of her gaze from Jay's body now. She wrapped it up in sheets from head to foot, the last one knotted tightly around the middle to give her a handhold.

She stood up and looked at the mummified figure that could leave no traces for police to find in the trunk of her car. She had moved outside the law; the police were not friends and protectors, they had become the enemy.

She wiped up bloodstains on the floor, rinsed the cloth under cold water and turned off the kitchen lights before she stepped outside to glance over at the apartment. Just one light turned on, the garage door open on emptiness. Gretchen Addison—but for how much longer?—was still at the laundromat.

Mrs. Mercer unlocked her car trunk, raised the lid and went back into the kitchen. The hard part lay ahead. As she grasped the handhold on the sheet she tried to divorce her mind from what her body, still strong and muscular, did. The mummified figure must not be thought of as a young man alive so short a time ago, but only as a heavy, awkward object that she had to get out to her car.

Somehow she accomplished it, pushing, pulling over the threshold, across the back porch, bumping it down the steps while her truant emotions kept changing it back from an object into the body of Jay Addison, dead by her hand.

Object, she reminded herself again, panting and pulling on the short stretch of flagstone walk to the driveway. Object she had to dispose of to save herself.

At last she got it to the car and propped it up against the open trunk. As she paused then to catch her breath, a car slowing down out front put her through a moment of terror, conjuring up the image of Gretchen Addison's return, her headlights shining on the tableau of sheeted object, open trunk, Mrs. Mercer standing nearby.

The car went on past but the moment of terror galvanized Mrs. Mercer into instant action, all qualms dismissed as she shoved Jay's body headlong into the trunk, tumbled the lower part in by the legs and slammed the lid shut.

She ran back to the house, turned on the kitchen light, stripped off the raincoat. A trip to the downstairs bathroom came next to wash her hands, smooth her hair and inspect herself in the full-length mirror for signs of her ordeal.

Her face seemed a little gaunter with a gray look under the tan but that was all. She rubbed her cheeks and put on lipstick.

Back then to the kitchen for a last quick survey of it. The gun went into her pocketbook to be locked up in the

Only Couples Need Apply

glove compartment. There was nothing else that wouldn't pass muster except for the contents of Jay Addison's pockets spread out on the table.

She looked at them, hesitated over the wallet, then opened it to remove his money, driver's license, and other identification.

There was none. No credit cards—that was strange—not even one from a gas company which most car owners had. No pictures, no papers of any sort, just the driver's license and twenty-six dollars in bills. Or so it seemed at first until she discovered the secret compartment that held ten one-hundred-dollar bills. She fanned them out on the table. Ten of them. Why should Jay Addison carry a thousand dollars in cash around with him? What use would he have for it? He had a checking account here in Belmont, paid his rent and presumably other bills by check and could draw out cash in smaller amounts as he needed it.

One thousand dollars . . .

But there wasn't time to puzzle over that now.

Mrs. Mercer put his belongings in a paper bag to be locked up in the glove compartment with the gun. She collected her pocketbook, keys, and housewarming gift. She turned the overhead kitchen light off, the porch light on and was starting out the back door when the thought struck her that someone might try to call her later tonight when she was supposed to be home. She took the phone off the hook.

Reaction set in as she got into her car. She shook from head to foot, faint from exhaustion.

She put her head down on her arms, crossing them on the steering wheel and drawing in deep breaths of the cool night air.

In a few moments she felt better. She lifted her head and glanced at the house. It looked so normal. Night light burning in the kitchen, back porch light on according to her habit.

Gretchen Addison, poor girl, who didn't know yet that she was a widow, would see nothing amiss when she returned from the laundromat.

Except that her husband wouldn't be waiting for her there in the apartment.

No use thinking of that.

Mrs. Mercer started her car and backed down the driveway.

She didn't know how she was to get through the party. She only knew that somehow she would.

16

She almost hit a parked car on the way as she swerved across the road to avoid running over a broken bottle that might have cut her tire. The last thing she could afford right now was to have a flat. Not because she didn't know how to change it, but for fear someone would stop to help her if she started changing it herself.

She slowed down fixing her attention on the road.

The party was in full swing when she arrived, cars lined up in the driveway and along the curb in front of the house.

Mrs. Mercer parked at the head of the line, picked up the two packages on the seat beside her and walked back to the brightly lighted entrance.

Voices and laughter poured out the open doorway. Mrs. Mercer apologized for her lateness and presented the two gifts.

"But what kept you, Anna?" someone asked presently, offering a drink.

"Oh, all sorts of complications. Take me all night to tell you about them."

She felt as if she were two people, one half of her seemingly attuned to the party that eddied and swirled around her, the other half totally removed, immersed in the bleak aftermath that lay ahead.

She kept track of the time. At ten-thirty she sought out her hostess and said, "I'm afraid I've got to leave now."

"Oh no, Anna," her hostess protested. "You mustn't miss the marvelous supper the girls have planned for later. They brought all the food themselves—"

Only Couples Need Apply

"Only I couldn't touch it," Mrs. Mercer said. "Something I had for dinner—the fish, probably—upset my stomach. That's what made me so late. I began to feel queasy driving over to Janet's and when I got back home I was so sick to my stomach that I felt for a while as if I couldn't come at all."

"But why didn't you say—?"

"No need to make a fuss. But if you don't mind, I'll just slip out quietly now."

"Of course not." Her hostess gave her a concerned look. "You do look a little pale at that, Anna. You sure you feel up to driving yourself home?"

"Oh yes. As soon as I get there I'll go straight to bed. I'll call you tomorrow."

"In the meantime, though, if there's anything I can do—"

"Thank you, I'm sure I'll be all right," Mrs. Mercer made an unobtrusive exit.

Almost from the start she had known what she was going to do with Jay Addison's body, the place springing into her mind, an abandoned eighteenth-century farmhouse, on a country road near the Belmont town line. Coming back from lunch somewhere a few years ago with her sister and brother-in-law, who found old houses irresistible, nothing would do but that they explore it, broken windows, sagging roof, overgrown garden and all.

It could still be salvaged, her brother-in-law said, but not much longer; unless someone got to work on it within the next two or three years it would be too late.

No one had. Mrs. Mercer remembered glancing at it when she happened to be over that way not long ago, thinking that it looked more derelict than ever.

Somewhere in the underbrush in back of the house she would leave Jay Addison's body.

At nearly eleven o'clock at night there was little traffic on the country road that led to it. She drove slowly watching for the turn into the lane. Although there were no other cars in sight when she came to it, she switched off her headlights as she made the turn and then crawled up the weed-choked lane in low gear with just her parking lights on.

The lane ended in back of the house at a small open shed with tire marks visible in the beaten-down grass around it. Recent ones, Mrs. Mercer thought, eyeing them uneasily. Couples, probably, parking.

She could only hope there'd be none tonight. She backed her car around in the tall grass to head it outward. Then, flashlight in hand, she searched around in the underbrush for a spot offering adequate cover for the body.

But not for long, she realized, as she flashed her light around. Aside from the parking couples, there was a patch of woodland nearby to attract children; and the pond down the road where fishermen would come. Which was just as well. For Gretchen Addison's sake, she didn't want the body left unfound for more than a few days, just long enough to blur the sequence of tonight's events and make it impossible to pinpoint the time of death.

It was a little easier to drag the body out of the trunk than it had been to get it in. Even so, it was a difficult task, the tall grass wet with dew, Mrs. Mercer soaked to the knees before she finally got the body out of sight, casual sight, at least, in the underbrush.

She was frightened the whole time, nerves on edge, heart leaping over every night sound of the countryside; the sudden chirp of a cricket right under her feet, the rustle of some small creature moving through the underbrush, the plaintive call of a whippoorwill.

She hadn't thought to bring scissors to cut away the sheets. She broke two fingernails tugging at the knots in them, unwinding and pulling them out from under the inert body, just beginning to stiffen. All she wanted was to be done with it, free of the grisly object that had brought her to this dark and lonely place.

There was still the empty wallet. She wiped it off and threw it into the underbrush well away from the body but near enough for the police to find.

It was over at last, the bloodstained sheets bundled into the trunk, she driving down the lane, turning out onto the road, switching her lights from parking to low beam.

She stopped twice on the country road, throwing the penknife and handkerchief into a ditch in one place, the driver's license in another.

Then there was only the gun—she would never touch one again as long as she lived—to get rid of.

When she took care of that, there'd be nothing left to connect her with Jay Addison's death.

Only Couples Need Apply 111

Except, of course, their landlady-tenant relationship.

Even that didn't involve her much. She could say quite truthfully—and Gretchen Addison would bear her out—that she'd had little contact with them all summer. The night he disappeared? Yes, she had seen him outside on her way to a party. He had mentioned going for a walk—which got him off the premises—and that was the last she had seen of him.

How soon would Gretchen Addison report him missing to the police?

Mrs. Mercer followed a circuitous route home that took her past the reservoir. She pulled up close to the guardrail, got out of her car and threw the gun as far out as she could into the water.

It was midnight when she arrived home. She saw the lights still on out in back as she turned in at the driveway. Naturally, she thought. Gretchen Addison waiting up for her husband, no idea yet, poor girl, that she would wait in vain.

Mrs. Mercer stopped near her back door, took the bundle of bloodstained sheets out of the trunk and carried them inside to the utility room. She ran cold water in the washer, added bleach and detergent, and put the sheets to soak.

Then she went back out to her car and drove it into the garage.

Gretchen came downstairs as she was closing the garage door and voiced the inevitable question, "Did you see my husband tonight, Mrs. Mercer, before you went out?"

"Yes, just as I was leaving. A little before eight."

"Oh ..." Gretchen hesitated. "Did he mention going anywhere? He wasn't home, you see, when I got back around ten o'clock and I can't think where he'd be all this time. I had the car so it doesn't seem as if he could go very far—"

There was no mistaking the genuine anxiety, the tension in Gretchen's voice. Mrs. Mercer, her ear attuned to any false note, felt that she could absolve the younger woman of playing a part in her husband's activities that night.

"Well, when I spoke to him he said he might go for a walk," Mrs. Mercer paused and then, feeling she should offer some sympathetic comment, added, "Perhaps he ran into someone he knew and they're just sitting around somewhere talking and have lost track of the time."

How awful of me, she thought a moment later. How could I say that?

Gretchen looked away from her. "That's probably what happened," she said. "Jay should be along any minute." She turned toward the stairs. "Good night, Mrs. Mercer."

"Good night." Mrs. Mercer crossed the yard with dragging step instead of her usual brisk tread. She felt old and worn. She went straight up to bed.

She looked out her rear window when she had turned off the light. Gretchen Addison's lights were still on while she waited up for her husband who would never come home again.

At least she would never know now that she was married to a thief, a potential killer, Mrs. Mercer told herself, trying to ease pangs of guilt.

A little later, lying wakeful in the dark, she heard Gretchen drive out. Gone to look for her husband in whatever bars or restaurants were still open at this time of night.

Mrs. Mercer, who almost never cried, suddenly found herself in tears and wept until she fell into the sleep of total exhaustion.

Gretchen hadn't been concerned over Jay's absence when she arrived home from the laundromat. She felt annoyed that he wasn't there to help her carry the clean laundry upstairs and even more annoyed over his carelessness in leaving their door unlocked. He had gone for a walk, she thought at first, as he had two or three times lately, and was probably in some bar within walking distance.

She put the laundry away, made herself a drink and sat down to watch the ten o'clock news. But when eleven o'clock came and went with no sign of him, she began to feel uneasy. He had never stayed away this late before.

Uneasiness turned to anger after she had talked with Mrs. Mercer. He had got drunk in some bar, picked up a girl . . .

Gretchen walked the floor. The fool, the stupid idiot, talking, bragging somewhere about God only knew what.

Only Couples Need Apply

Go and look for him. Cover as many bars as she could before they all closed for the night.

It was past two o'clock when she returned. Mrs. Mercer's house, every house on the street was in darkness. The only lights visible were those she had left on in the apartment. She climbed the stairs, trying to convince herself that Jay had come home during her absence but knowing, with alarm bells ringing inside her after her futile trip, that he had not, that the note she had left on the table, *Gone out looking for you, back soon,* would still be there unread.

Gretchen wandered through the empty confines of the three rooms until she was assailed by the new and devastating thought that he might have run out on her.

She flew to the kitchen scrabbling through her key case for the key that unlocked their strongbox, pushed far back out of sight in the storage chest. It was still there and their various bankbooks and traveler's checks were still in it. The checkbook for their joint account was in her pocketbook, her key to their safe deposit box in New Haven in a separate compartment. He kept his with his other keys in a bureau drawer. She went to look. It was still there with the rest.

Jay had not run out on her, not rented a car or taken a bus anywhere. The only money he had with him that amounted to anything was his emergency fund.

There was no emergency, though, no reason at all for him to take off. The only explanation left was that he had got so drunk with whatever girl he picked up that he had gone to her place to spend the night.

Gretchen might as well go to bed herself.

17

Toward morning she fell asleep; not the sleep of total exhaustion that had overtaken Mrs. Mercer but a series of catnaps broken by half-waking intervals that brought awareness of Jay's absence.

At seven she was suddenly wide awake looking out at the freshness of the morning angry once again at Jay for daring to treat her like this but uneasy, too, at the thought that he was now nearly twelve hours unaccounted for. No matter how drunk he'd got, he had never done anything like this before, never gone home with some girl overnight.

Gretchen got up and went into the bathroom. She splashed cold water on her face, brushed her hair, studied her reflection in the mirror, the drawn look she had, the circles under her eyes. She would be twenty-nine soon and this morning she looked every day of it. Jay's fault, bastard that he was.

She made a pot of coffee, carried her cup into the living room and turned on the seven-thirty local news. No mention of an unidentified young man found injured or dead by the roadside. How could Jay be unidentified, anyway, when he had his driver's license with him?

She cooked breakfast and forced herself to eat it although she had no appetite.

She felt a little better after a shower. She flew to answer the phone when it rang at nine o'clock—Jay, of course, waking up wherever he was with a terrible hangover and calling to offer some phony excuse or other.

But it was Mrs. Mercer, up even earlier than Gretchen but waiting until what seemed a civilized hour to call about Jay, not wanting to yet knowing she should.

"Oh," said Gretchen on a falling note when she heard her voice. "Good morning."

Only Couples Need Apply

"Good morning, Mrs. Addison. I've been wondering if your husband got home all right."

"No, I haven't seen or heard from him. Whoever he met last night, he must have done some heavy drinking, I'm afraid, and is sleeping it off somewhere." Gretchen kept her tone light. "You know how men act sometimes when they're out from under their wives' thumbs."

"Well, yes . . ." replied Mrs. Mercer who had never had that sort of experience with her own husband. She felt relieved that Gretchen wasn't ready to call the police right away but at the same time taken aback by her contained attitude. The young these days were much more casual than her generation had ever been, she realized, but even so . . .

"I hope you'll hear from him soon, Mrs. Addison," she said.

"Oh, I imagine so. In fact, I thought it must be Jay when you called."

"Well then, I'd better hang up and leave your line free." The next moment Mrs. Mercer heard herself add, "It's just as well to wait, I guess. It would be too bad to call the police and then have it turn out to be unnecessary."

Police. What on earth had made her bring that up, the last thing she should have mentioned?

"Police?" There was a brief silence at Gretchen's end as the enormity of involving them, all that it would entail, sank into her mind.

"Oh no," she replied presently. "It's much too soon for that. I'm sure I'll hear from Jay before long."

"Well, do let me know."

"Yes, I will, Mrs. Mercer. Thank you, for calling."

Gretchen hung up and reached for her cigarettes. Police, she thought. God. Of all the things she couldn't do to find Jay, that was it.

The morning wore on. No word from him. She heard Mrs. Mercer drive out of the garage. Nothing on her mind, probably, but her grocery list.

When eleven o'clock, twelve, came and went with no word from Jay, Gretchen revised the duration of last night's binge. It must have been an all-night affair. Jay might not sleep it off until late afternoon.

She fell asleep herself on the sofa after lunch and didn't wake up until four o'clock. She looked at her watch. It was now over twenty hours since Jay had dropped out of sight. No matter who he'd picked up or how drunk he'd got last night he wouldn't have let the whole day go by without getting in touch with her. Something had happened to him . . .

But what? Nothing to do with the police or they would have been on the doorstep long ago.

Someone from out of the past recognizing him, sending him into hiding?

No. Anything like that, Jay, even on the run so as not to lead them here, would have managed to phone her.

Could he have been killed by a car with the driver taking his body away somewhere to hide it?

No. Not out for a walk in this area where there were people around and a steady flow of traffic.

What in the world, then, could have happened to him?

No answer to the question came to her. Gretchen sought respite from it by turning her thoughts to what explanation she could give Mrs. Mercer for not reporting her husband missing to the police. Mrs. Mercer would think it was funny if she didn't call soon.

Gretchen concentrated, finally concocted a story that seemed plausible. She would enlarge on what she had said earlier about Jay's drinking last night; say that he sometimes went off on periodic binges. Not too often, but maybe three or four times a year; and that when he did, he vanished completely for several days.

It should satisfy Mrs. Mercer for the moment. Call her now and get it over with . . .

Mrs. Mercer listened in silence and then said, "What a shame, Mrs. Addison. Do you think he's somewhere here in town? He had no car."

"Oh, that wouldn't stop him. He could rent one or pick up someone in a bar to drive him." Gretchen sighed heavily. "He was restless yesterday. I should have seen the signs, not left him alone last night. But he's been on such good behavior all summer, I suppose I just let myself relax."

"How sad for both of you," Mrs. Mercer said. "Is there anything I can do to help?"

"No, thank you. It's just a matter of waiting for Jay to pull out of it and come home. Meanwhile"—Gretchen was thinking ahead now—"I'm going to try to keep things as

Only Couples Need Apply

normal as I can for myself. I was planning to visit a friend in Hartford tomorrow and I'll just go ahead with it."

"Yes, that's the best thing for you."

"I'll leave a note, although I'm sure Jay won't be back. It's always three or four days."

"Oh dear, I'm so sorry about it. Try to have a pleasant day."

Mrs. Mercer felt like a hypocrite as she hung up. On the other hand, what harm did it do to let the poor girl believe as long as she could that it was just one of her husband's sprees? She would have to face a far worse reality soon enough.

A moment later, thinking over what Gretchen had said, Mrs. Mercer wondered if Jay Addison's drinking habits explained the thousand dollars hidden in his wallet. It seemed an excessive amount, though, for just three or four days. To say nothing of the risk of being robbed of it.

Or was he the type to throw money around with both hands?

It was the only answer that made sense so far.

Surprising, though, she thought next, how well he had concealed his drinking problem. From her own limited observation of him, he had seemed to follow the normal pattern of social drinking.

But he hadn't seemed to be a thief, a potential murderer either...

Gretchen waited until six o'clock before she tried to contact Jay through the emergency procedure settled upon early in the summer. Then she went to a public phone and called the West Rock Motel in New Haven. "Can you tell me, please," she asked the desk clerk, "if Mr. John Collins has registered yet or made a reservation? This is Mrs. Collins speaking."

After a moment's wait the desk clerk returned to the phone. "No, ma'am, Mr. Collins isn't registered and we have no reservation for him. But would you care to leave a message or a number where he can reach you if he does arrive?"

"No, thank you, I'll call again later."

"Where in hell can the jerk be?" Gretchen muttered to herself, anger briefly overriding worry as she came out of the phone booth. "What's he got himself into?"

Nothing connected with the police. There was still that much consolation.

She went home, fixed herself a dinner of sorts, watched the news, local and national—no event, large or small, could have any bearing on Jay's disappearance—and at nine o'clock called the motel again. Mr. John Collins was still not registered.

"My God," she said aloud on the way home. "Where is he? What has he got mixed up in?"

Ruling out all connection with their projects, what was left?

The answer had been long in coming but now it stared her in the face; the emergency money Jay carried around with him.

He must have got drunk and flashed it around in front of the wrong people in some bar; and been talked into accepting a ride home with them or going on to another bar.

Then what?

They might have beaten him unconscious, dumped him out of the car anywhere. At this point he might be lying in a hospital, still unconscious, no identification on him once he was stripped of his wallet with his driver's license in it.

He might even be dead, his body left in some spot where days, weeks could go by before it was found.

Whatever mess he had got into was his own fault and had nothing to do with their partnership.

Which left Gretchen in a situation where she had better start looking after herself.

18

Decision made, she slept soundly that night and was up at seven Thursday morning, making plans for the day.

After breakfast she balanced their checkbook and arrived at a figure of $1855.25. She made out a check to cash for eighteen hundred. Their Belmont savings account

Only Couples Need Apply

had only seven hundred left in it; she would just close it out.

She thought about a new name for herself while she showered and dressed. Whatever she settled on she would keep indefinitely. There could be no more projects without Jay—unless she met someone like him—and she could hardly count on that. Use her own first name then ...

Gretchen Slocum became her choice.

She took the Hartford bankbooks out of the strongbox just before she left at nine o'clock, carrying a big pocketbook roomy enough to hold all the cash that would go into it later. Her first stop would be the Belmont banks; then she would drive to Hartford.

Mrs. Mercer, who hadn't slept well that night, was getting her breakfast when Gretchen left, making an early start, she thought, to spend the day with her friend in Hartford.

It seemed coldhearted to Mrs. Mercer. She felt that if she were in Gretchen Addison's place, she would at least wait another hour or so just in case her husband called sooner than she expected.

But perhaps it wasn't fair to make a judgment. Only she knew how bad her past experiences with Jay Addison's drinking had been.

The next moment Mrs. Mercer admitted to herself that she was glad to have her gone for the day. It was less harrowing than to picture her alone out there in the apartment waiting for a phone call that would never come.

Who was she visiting, though? Yesterday was the first reference she had ever made to any friend, least of all one no farther away than Hartford.

All summer, in that strange isolation they had insisted upon, they had at least had each other. Who would Gretchen Addison turn to now?

She must have relatives somewhere; and friends other than the one in Hartford. But no matter who there was, she had a hard time ahead of her, starting a new life for herself.

Suddenly, for the first time since she had killed him, Mrs. Mercer thought of Jay Addison's book. Now it would never be finished, no one would ever know how good it would have been.

Another thought—that it seemed out-of-character for a

thief to be writing a book at all—occurred to her. Or wasn't it? She had no knowledge of what had led to it.

Her phone rang, a friend asking if she would be free that evening to make a fourth for pot luck supper and bridge.

"Love to," Mrs. Mercer replied, pleased to escape her own company for a few hours.

"Good. Around six, shall we say? That will give us time for a couple of drinks before I start cooking the steaks outdoors."

"Sounds just fine."

Mrs. Mercer felt more cheerful when she hung up, the body in back of the farmhouse a little farther removed from her.

The house was still too quiet, too empty, though, as she moved about in her morning routine. She missed Billy so. She shrank from the thought of replacing him but maybe she should, now that her first grief over him was behind her . . .

Gretchen's pocketbook bulged with more than fifty thousand in cash when she had closed the tw bank accounts in Hartford, the tellers in each instance looking taken aback by her request for cash.

Other banks in the downtown area were conveniently close to each other. By one o'clock, going from one to another, she had converted most of the money into traveler's checks made out to Gretchen Slocum.

The day was hot. She had lunch in an air-conditioned restaurant, reviewing her assets during the meal. Thirty thousand in traveler's checks, over three thousand in cash, counting her emergency money; twenty-seven thousand more in New Haven, plus the jewelry. That presented a bit of a problem. Jay had always handled selling it in the past. She would have to take her time.

But then, she could afford to. The money would last twice as long without Jay to share it. Longer, in fact. He wanted to spend it all as fast as it came in, she was more careful with it.

Eventually, though, it would be gone. What would happen then if she hadn't found a partner to replace him?

Or should she even try? With the stake she had, she might look for a rich husband. No reason, with her looks, that she shouldn't find one.

Only Couples Need Apply

On the way home Gretchen gave thought to the tidying-up details that had to be taken care of before she left for good tomorrow. Television set to be returned—perhaps Mrs. Mercer would see to that—rent due from the first of September to the middle of the month when they were supposed to vacate the apartment. The extra month's deposit they had paid before they moved in would more than cover that. She certainly wouldn't worry about leaving a forwarding address to which the refund could be sent.

She got home at four-thirty but wasn't ready to face Mrs. Mercer yet.

Instead, she got out suitcases and began to pack, her own things first, then Jay's.

There were all the other things to pack too. The typewriter, manuscript—no way to burn it—the book it was copied from, linens, flatware, incidentals they had been acquiring all summer. A bore to have to get them all downstairs to the car but it wouldn't look right to leave them behind.

Gretchen hesitated over Jay's gun. She would have to take it with her and get rid of it later. He should have got rid of it himself long ago, the gun that had killed Mrs. Russell. He said he would; he said he wanted to replace it first, though, with one he liked as well, that he'd got so he would feel naked without one. But he had just let it go and now, she thought irritatedly, it was left to her.

Where should she pack it? Somewhere handier than the strongbox in case she found a convenient place to stop along the road. She finally hid it under one of her wigs.

At quarter of six, in the midst of her packing she heard Mrs. Mercer start her car up, back it out of the garage. She was headed down the driveway when Gretchen looked out the front window. She had turned her back porch light on which meant she wouldn't be back until after dark, perhaps not until it was too late for Gretchen to see her tonight.

Write a note then, drop it through her mail slot in the morning—much easier than a conversation that might include awkward questions.

Before nine o'clock she had the car packed, all but suitcases that wouldn't fit into the crammed trunk. She made a meal out of leftovers and cleaned out the refrigerator, meanwhile listening for Mrs. Mercer's car. There was no sign of it.

At ten o'clock when everything was done, the apartment put in order, Gretchen decided to make one more call to the West Rock Motel, even though it seemed that Jay would surely have called her by this time if he had ever arrived there.

She turned off all the lights before she left—let Mrs. Mercer, if she returned before her, think she had gone to bed early—and walked to a nearby phone booth.

No, the desk clerk said, Mr. John Collins still wasn't registered. He spoke with a slight smirk in his voice as if he thought she was a suspicious wife checking up on her husband.

He'd never know how far off the mark he was.

Mrs. Mercer hadn't come home in her absence. She got undressed in the dark, turning on a light just long enough to set her alarm for six o'clock. She went right to sleep and didn't hear Mrs. Mercer drive in around midnight.

Mrs. Mercer glanced up at her darkened windows, hoping she hadn't disturbed her rest. She felt a little guilty over what a pleasant evening she'd had herself, enjoying dinner and bridge with friends. There had been intervals when she hadn't even thought of Jay Addison or his wife who would begin by tomorrow to look for his return.

Her conscience troubled her, though, over her neglect of the poor girl since yesterday. She had thought of calling her after she got back from Hartford this afternoon but, not wanting to, had made up excuses to herself about Gretchen Addison taking her for a busybody if she did.

Tomorrow morning, first thing, she would.

19

Gretchen got out of bed the moment the alarm rang. She dressed, packed last-minute things and carried them down

Only Couples Need Apply

to the car, along with the strongbox and the suitcases that wouldn't fit in the trunk.

Her note to Mrs. Mercer came next. She made herself a cup of instant coffee and sat down at the desk. Wording it required thought even though she knew what she wanted to say. The first attempt didn't satisfy her. She tore it into small pieces and burned them in the sink. The second seemed better, had a more natural sound. She put it in an envelope with a ten-dollar bill and laid it beside her pocketbook.

She donned gloves for the final chore of wiping off fingerprints. Not because there was any real need of it, any prospect of the police showing up to look for them as they had after the projects but because it had become part of the routine of shedding one identity before adopting another. It was, at the very least, a precaution that could do no harm.

She had begun it yesterday with her packing, methodically wiping off every object or surface she would have no occasion to touch again. Now there were left just those she had come in contact with that morning, windows as she closed them, desk, faucets, doorknobs, whatever might have retained her prints.

She hurried toward the end. It was seven-thirty. Mrs. Mercer would soon be up and about. A few minutes later, Gretchen locked the apartment door after her for the last time and put the two sets of house keys into the envelope.

It was a gray humid morning. Gretchen heard a distant rumble of thunder as she stopped her car abreast of Mrs. Mercer's front door. She walked very quietly up the steps and slid the envelope through the mail slot. A moment later she was back in her car and on her way.

Mrs. Mercer, just as she got out of bed, heard Gretchen's car in the driveway and wondered where she could be going so early in the morning. When she heard the rattle of the mail slot she looked again at her bedroom clock to verify that it was only twenty of eight. Early for the mailman, she thought. He never arrived much before nine. She didn't connect the two separate sounds until she went downstairs a few minutes later and saw the unstamped envelope lying on the rug just inside the door.

"Now what can this be?" she said aloud. She picked it up, heavy with the weight of the keys, opened it, took out

Gretchen's note and sat down at the hall table with it, putting back the ten-dollar bill enclosed.

Dear Mrs. Mercer [she read],

I had a phone call last night from a man who said he was an old friend of Jay's and that Jay was with him, had been drinking heavily and was in some sort of trouble. He gave me the name of a motel outside of Hartford where I'm to meet Jay this morning. He also said that Jay wanted me to bring him some clothes since we'll have to go to New York for several days to straighten out this trouble he's in.

When I thought it all over, it seemed so confusing that I decided it was best not to make plans for coming back here—considering that we were to vacate the apartment, anyway, by the middle of September—so I packed all our things last night and got them into the car ready to leave first thing this morning.

I'm sorry not to say good-by but the call came much too late for me to call you last night and I didn't want to wake you when I left this morning.

I'm enclosing the keys to the apartment and ten dollars that should cover the phone bill. Will you please call the TV people to pick up the set we were renting? It's paid for until the first of the month. Regarding the apartment, the deposit we made when we took it should cover the half-month's rent due for September. In any case, I'll call you within the next week or so and if there's anything I've overlooked, we can straighten it out then.

Thank you for helping to make the summer so pleasant. We've both enjoyed knowing you and hope to see you again sometime.

Sincerely,
Gretchen Addison

Mrs. Mercer read the note twice, then went back to the first part of it for the third time in stunned bewilderment. A friend of Jay Addison's saying that he was with him and that he was in some sort of trouble. Saying he was at a motel outside of Hartford. Saying he was alive . . .

Only Couples Need Apply

She put the note aside and stood up. She needed a cup of coffee before she could even try to collect her thoughts. Jay Addison supposed to be at a motel outside of Hartford, his wife on her way to meet him there ...

Two cups of coffee later Mrs. Mercer could still make no sense of it. Why should this old friend of Jay Addison's pretend he was with him—of course the friend didn't know, no one but herself knew he was dead—but still, why should he have called Mrs. Addison right at this particular time with a story like that?

Mrs. Mercer had a slice of toast with her third cup of coffee. Another question occurred to her—assuming some sort of hoax or, even worse, confidence game—how had the man known Jay Addison had been missing the past few days?

She picked up the note again. " ... from a man who said he was an old friend of Jay's ..." Who said. Apparently, not anyone Gretchen Addison had ever heard of herself or she would have worded it differently.

But what was the point to the whole thing? What was she walking into?

The more Mrs. Mercer puzzled over it, the less meaning it had. Except that presently it began to take on implications of something that might be dangerous to the girl.

If there were only some way to get in touch with her. A motel outside of Hartford, but no name, no clue to its location.

What good would it do, anyway, if she could reach her? She could hardly tell her that the message was a hoax, that her husband couldn't be at any motel because Mrs. Mercer had killed him the other night and left his body in back of an old farmhouse.

There was nothing she could do, in fact, except to go on puzzling, worrying, over what it all meant.

She went upstairs. While she was getting dressed, the sky darkened, the rumbles of thunder came closer. There was going to be a storm soon. It might break before Gretchen Addison reached the motel outside of Hartford.

Presently, Mrs. Mercer went out to the apartment and walked from room to room, opening cupboard and closet doors aimlessly, finding everything in perfect order—but then, hadn't she congratulated herself last spring on her new tenant being neat as a pin?—an empty shell that told her nothing.

The storm broke soon after she got back home, lightning, thunder, torrents of rain. At least, she thought, looking out at the downpour, it would wash away any traces, tire tracks or whatever, her car might have left at the farmhouse.

The young couple approaching it at the height of the storm were thinking only of shelter as they got wetter and wetter riding in an ancient convertible with a sieve-like canvas top.

"Look," the girl cried, ducking from one leak to another and pointing to the farmhouse ahead. "Let's stop there."

The young man turned in onto the lane, bumped along it, pulling up as close as he could get to the shed out in back.

They dashed inside and mopped themselves off as best they could with his handkerchief, laughing over their bedraggled state.

After another ten or fifteen minutes the storm spent itself. The young man went out to his car and tried to mop up the pools of water on the seat with his soggy handkerchief. The girl joined in on his rueful exclamations. She didn't have a handkerchief herself; she could only offer a handful of damp tissues that were no help at all.

Suddenly the sun came out. The young man put the top down to let the seat dry out. "We'll wait a few minutes," he said.

The girl kicked off her loafers and walked barefoot around the yard through the tall grass flattened by wind and rain.

Presently her wandering took her farther out in back where the underbrush, like the grass, had been beaten down by the storm.

The girl looked casually at a tangled clump of it, looked again, whirled around and ran back to the young man.

"Oh, come quick," she said in a small frightened voice, "there's something—someone—lying out there."

The time was eleven o'clock.

20

At three that afternoon Sergeant Tripp and Officer Yorke of the Belmont police began an examination of the dank-smelling clothes removed from the dead man.

They handled them carefully, knowing they might have to be sent to the state police laboratory later for tests the Belmont police were not equipped to make themselves.

All they knew so far about the dead man was that he was a white male, blond, probably in his late twenties, and had apparently died of a bullet wound three or four days earlier. No one matching his description had been reported missing; the police were inclined to think he might not be a local man.

They would know more about him before the day was out. The pathologist at Belmont Hospital, feeling put-upon under pressure from them, had scheduled the autopsy for four-thirty that afternoon.

Meanwhile, the clothes were all they really had to work with. Nothing much was expected from the search now in progress at the farmhouse; the downpour that morning had obliterated any traces of the crime, except for the empty wallet, already found.

"Guy wasn't on relief," Sergeant Tripp remarked. "Good quality stuff, underwear and all."

"Pierre Cardin," Yorke said, looking at the label. After a moment's thought, he added, "Wonder if he bought it at Bretten's. Only men's shop around here that carries them."

"How can you be sure of that?" the sergeant demanded. "Must be a dozen or more of them in town."

Yorke, twenty-six, unmarried, clothes-conscious, replied firmly, "Not good ones. Not more than three or four. I've bought in all of them, that's how I know. And Bretten's is the best."

"Most expensive, that's for sure," muttered Tripp who at thirty-seven with a wife and three children to support, had never set foot in Bretten's himself. "Put the shirt in a plastic bag, though, and we'll try them. How about the slacks?"

"Brooks Brothers?" Yorke queried on a patient note. "Not around here."

"All right," Tripp snapped, to put his subordinate, getting above himself, in his place, "We'll take the shirt over right now."

Their arrival at Bretten's, discreet as it was, plainclothes and unmarked car, caused a flurry of interest. The few salesmen—the shop featured quality rather than quantity—put their heads together with Bretten, the owner, refreshing each other's memory on what customers had bought that particular shirt, eliminating most of them by name. Presently one of the salesmen recalled selling a striped Cardin shirt, possibly blue and green, to a young fellow who had bought a gray cord suit the same day.

"That's why I remember it," he added. "Not much demand for gray cords this summer. Bright colors are more popular."

"Bunch of peacocks," said Tripp, whose own drab out-of-date attire had already drawn pitying glances from the staff. "How about your fitter? Pants had to be measured for length."

Bretten, a modified peacock himself in mauve suit and shirt, and pink-flowered tie, nodded, "Yes, of course," he said, and sent for the fitter.

The fitter retained a vague memory of the gray cord suit. "Only two all summer, think of that," he said. "One of them was early in the season because the other one, on sale last month, was bought by one of our regulars, Mr. Harvey Fuller, and needed quite a few alterations. He's a heavy-set man, you see, broader in the hips than the shoulders, and it's a problem, altering his clothes to fit properly—"

"The other one, Griffith," Bretten broke in, aware of the long-suffering look on Sergeant Tripp's face.

"Oh yes, the one early in the season. May or June, I think. Let me just go check my records..."

The sergeant and Yorke resigned themselves to a long wait but the fitter was back in a few minutes looking pleased with himself. "Early, like I thought," he said. "June 3, picked up June 4. Jay Addison, the slip shows.

Only Couples Need Apply

Comes back to me now, young man, blond, looked real good in the suit."

The police officers pricked up their ears. No description of the corpse had been given to the fitter. Perhaps they had a lead, after all.

"Could I see your phone book?" the sergeant asked Bretten.

"Certainly." Bretten took them to his private office and withdrew.

Samuel W. was the only Addison listed.

"Try information for a new listing," Tripp directed his subordinate.

Yorke dialed for information, asked about the listing, scribbled a name and address and hung up.

"J. Addison—just the initial—519½ Lakeview Avenue," he said.

"Hmm." Tripp looked thoughtful. "Mrs. Mercer's place. She shot a kid who broke into her house—years ago before your time on the force—and since then, seems to me, she's fixed up an apartment out back."

The sergeant looked at his watch. "Get Dr. Reilly at the hospital. Ask him not to start the autopsy until he hears from me."

"He'll be mad as hell," Yorke said. "He didn't want to do it until tomorrow anyway."

"Too bad. Tell him it'll be just long enough to try for an identification."

A few minutes later they arrived at Mrs. Mercer's, going up the driveway past her house to stop outside the apartment. J. Addison, they read on the card in the nameplate and rang the bell.

"Let's try out front," said the sergeant when it went unanswered.

Mrs. Mercer was braced for them, having heard that Jay's body was found—unidentified body, the radio report said—on the one o'clock news. She felt relief as well as apprehension over their arrival. At least that peculiar business of the man calling Gretchen Addison could .be brought out into the open.

Sergeant Tripp and she remembered each other from that other time five years ago. He introduced his colleague. "Officer Yorke, Mrs. Mercer. We're making inquiries about your tenant, Mr. Addison, but no one seems to be home back there."

"No, they've given up the apartment. But do come in," She took them into the living room.

"When did they leave?" Tripp asked as soon as they were seated.

"He left first. Let me see, this is Friday..." She paused as if she had to give it thought to remember. "Tuesday night. Quite unexpectedly. Mrs. Addison left this morning."

"Unexpectedly..." Tripp ruminated. "What did Addison look like, Mrs. Mercer?"

"Well, good-looking young man, Sergeant. About five-ten, blond hair, well-built—"

"Uh-huh." Tripp stole a glance at his watch. Dr. Reilly would have a fit if they held him up much longer. "Did you hear any news reports, Mrs. Mercer, about the man's body found this morning?"

"The one who was shot? Yes, but they didn't say who it was."

"They didn't say because no identification has been made yet."

"Oh..." Mrs. Mercer let her voice trail off, her eyes widen as she stared at Tripp. "You don't mean—you don't think—?"

"I don't know yet." The sergeant stood up, Yorke following suit. "Have to ask you to go over to the hospital with us, Mrs. Mercer, to see if you can identify the body."

"Identify—?" Her dismay was the only genuine emotion she had shown since their arrival. How many people who killed someone had to identify the body afterward? It was the last thing she was prepared for.

"I'm afraid there's no choice, Mrs. Mercer."

No choice. She stood up reluctantly. "I'll just get my pocketbook..."

Pocketbook, thought Yorke. Why couldn't women stir out of the house without one?

There was no discussion of Jay on the drive to the hospital. The identification took no time at all.

"It's Mr. Addison," she said when the body was shown to her.

"All yours now, Dr. Reilly," Tripp said, and received a cold stare in return.

Only Couples Need Apply 131

Before they left the hospital, the sergeant called headquarters to report to Lieutenant Vaughan, in charge of the investigation, that the corpse was identified. Wheels would now start turning to check out Jay Addison.

Back at Mrs. Mercer's, seated once again in her living room, Tripp began, "You told us earlier, Mrs. Mercer, that Addison left unexpectedly—Tuesday night, you said?"

"Yes." Mrs. Mercer went through the story of seeing Jay outside as she was leaving to go to a party, his wife waiting to ask about him when she returned around midnight, what she had said the next day about her husband's drinking habits.

"She seem worried?"

"Not really. Resigned would be more like it." Mrs. Mercer spoke with more assurance now that she had got past the night she had killed Jay. But the next moment Sergeant Tripp cut the ground from under her by asking, "By the way, ma'am, where was the party you went to that night?"

She supplied details, a little daunted as she noticed the younger officer writing them down in the notebook he had produced at the start of her story. She wasn't, it seemed clear of suspicion herself. Well, of course not. Sergeant Tripp hadn't forgotten Hank Morrison's death. And now Jay Addison was dead of a bullet wound.

They would check her thoroughly, no doubt about that. Get it all in first herself . . .

She began with her stop at Janet Parker's, the latter's phone call from her son, her own realization that she had forgotten her housewarming gift and her return home for it.

"Any sign of Addison when you got back here?"

Mrs. Mercer shook her head. "I wasn't even thinking about him because I felt queasy all of a sudden on the way back. The fish I ate for dinner that night, I think. I barely made it to the bathroom before I threw up. I thought I wouldn't be able to go to the party at all but I took some baking soda and after a while I felt better and finally went. I didn't stay too long, though. The queasy feeling came back so I decided the best thing for me to do was to go home to bed."

"What time was that, Mrs. Mercer?"

"I didn't really notice. Perhaps around eleven or so."

There was still the second time gap to cover, in case anyone had noticed exactly when she left the party. It led her to add. "As a matter of fact, I got sick to my stomach again on the way and had to stop by the side of the road. Then I just sat there in my car until I felt sure I could drive the rest of the way home."

"So the last time you saw Addison alive was when you first left your house a little before eight?"

"Yes."

"Did Mrs. Addison mention what time she got back from the laundromat and found her husband gone?"

"She may have," Mrs. Mercer replied. "I don't really remember." The vaguer she was about time the better.

She went on to Gretchen's trip to Hartford the day before to visit a friend and then to her own activities last night, dinner and bridge, the apartment in darkness when she arrived home around midnight.

"So you see, I didn't talk to Mrs. Addison at all yesterday," she added. "I was just getting up when I heard her leaving at quarter of eight this morning and then found a note she had slipped through the mail slot when I came downstairs—oh, the note! How could I have forgotten it? It must have been the shock of hearing about Mr. Addison. I don't understand it at all, now that I know he's dead. Just let me get it—"

Mrs. Mercer hurried out to the kitchen where she had put the note away in a drawer. She brought it back and handed it to the sergeant.

The sergeant read it, passed it on to Yorke to read and began issuing orders to him. "Call Lieutenant Vaughan—if it's all right to use your phone, Mrs. Mercer?—and bring him up to date on developments here. Find out if he was able to get any information from local banks or the credit bureau before they closed. Not much to give him, a motel outside of Hartford, but he'll still want to start checking registrations to see if Mrs. Addison signed in at any of them today."

The tempo began to pick up as Yorke went to the phone. Tripp frowned over the note, firing questions at Mrs. Mercer about the Addisons, their general background, where they came from, what had brought them to Belmont, how long they had been renting the apartment, who their friends were and so on.

Only Couples Need Apply

The meagerness of her knowledge was embarrassing to disclose with Tripp's gimlet eye fixed on her. She kept reverting to the book Jay Addison was writing as the reason for the secluded life they had led all summer but Tripp, with the chronic suspicion of a cop, wasn't impressed.

"Never struck you they might be hiding out, Mrs. Mercer?"

"Oh no, Sergeant. They seemed a nice young couple."

Yorke, hanging up the phone in the kitchen, called, "Speak to you, Sergeant?"

Tripp went out to him. Mrs. Mercer, straining her ears, caught fragments of what Yorke said. Something about Mrs. Addison closing out accounts in local banks, taking the money, over two thousand, in cash.

Naturally, she'd close bank accounts, leaving Belmont for good. That much in cash, though, did seem odd.

Tripp asked for a key to the apartment. The next thing Mrs. Mercer knew, a police van was turning in at the driveway.

Later, after she had allowed her fingerprints to be taken for comparison purposes, she learned that hers were the only ones found in the apartment.

21

Gretchen stopped for breakfast on her way out of Belmont that morning. The storm caught her still east of Hartford forcing her, like most of the other cars on the highway, over onto the shoulder to wait out the worst of it.

Staring out at the cascade of rain she weighed the pros and cons of spending the night at the West Rock Motel in case, just in case, Jay tried to reach her there.

She didn't owe it to him; she had already kept her part of the bargain, given him plenty of time to get in touch with her, tried to call him three times herself at the motel.

She had every right to go straight on to New York after she had picked up the rest of the money and the jewelry, settle into her new identity and make plans for her future. Then it would be just a question of how long it would take her to find a rich husband.

If she really wanted one. There would be drawbacks to it. She would always have to be on guard against the past and might not be free, as she was now, to cut and run if any part of it ever threatened her. She would be making a commitment of sorts to a new kind of life; one that she might even find a bit boring, at best, after the challenges and risks the projects had involved.

Without Jay, though, how could she go on with them? For all his faults, it would be difficult to replace him.

Nothing to lose then, by staying over at the West Rock Motel, giving him one more chance to contact her . . .

She called the motel from downtown New Haven and reserved a room. "Mrs. John Collins," she said, adding without hope, "Has my husband made a reservation with you yet?"

"Just a moment . . . No, he hasn't."

"Well, thank you."

God, what had happened to Jay?

Gretchen put him out of her mind on her way to the New Haven bank. She took the jewelry and cash out of the safe deposit box and closed the savings account, asking for the money and accrued interest in cash.

The rest of the procedure was the same as yesterday's in Hartford, going to different banks to convert the cash into traveler's checks made out to Gretchen Slocum.

She would sell the car in New York, she reflected on her way back to it. Wherever she decided to go next, she would buy another car and get a driver's license in her new name.

She would then invest some of the money. Actually, with no new projects in sight, she could invest it as Gretchen Rowland if she wanted to.

How long since she had used her own last name? It took a moment's thought. Not since the Sherman project.

She stopped for a late lunch before she went to the motel, selecting a window table where she could keep an eye on her car with the strongbox locked up now in the trunk.

The same thought was in her mind when she left her

Only Couples Need Apply

car right outside the motel entrance while she checked in. The desk clerk, not the night man she had talked to on the phone, showed no interest in her.

Gretchen paid for her room in advance, explaining that she might want to make a very early start in the morning.

The room assigned to her was in a courtyard away from street traffic. It was on the second floor with a balcony overlooking the swimming pool. Gretchen thought of going for a swim but would not leave the strongbox unguarded. In any event, she reminded herself, she hadn't packed a suit in the overnight case that was the only other piece of luggage she had brought up to the room.

It was a long narrow room that ran the full depth of the building with a window opposite the balcony that gave her a view of her car parked directly below. It was locked up tight but she preferred having it where she could keep an eye on it from time to time.

She left a gap in the curtains to make it easier to glance out at it. Her nerves were on edge, she realized, but why not, considering all she had gone through these past three days?

A drink would do her good. She had a bottle of scotch in her suitcase. She rang room service for club soda and ice. She paid the boy who brought them, just as she had paid for her room in advance. If anything came up that she had to leave suddenly, she wanted no bill to delay her at the desk.

Not that anything could come up except a call from Jay. No one else, no one in Belmont, no one anywhere knew she was here at this motel registered as Mrs. John Collins. The persistent feeling she had that something might go wrong was just another sign of her nerves acting up.

She tossed off her first drink, scotch on the rocks, added soda to the second one and took it out on the balcony, pausing on the way to pick up a paperback she had bought in the motel lobby.

Stretched out on the chaise lounge with her drink and her book, Gretchen gradually relaxed and at last fell asleep.

Twilight was setting in when she woke up. She couldn't believe she had slept so long but she felt better for it, going back into the room and over to the window to look out and assure herself that her car was still right there below.

There was a menu on the bureau. She studied it and phoned room service to order dinner. She had a drink while she waited for it and turned on the TV but was too late for the news, catching just the tag end of it.

She paid for her dinner when it arrived, tipped the waiter and bolted and chained the door after him.

She took her time over the meal, watching a TV program even though it didn't interest her. Then she had to unchain, unbolt the door to put the tray outside. It was a nuisance but her meticulous sense of order wouldn't permit dirty dishes kept in the room.

She got undressed, hanging up her doubleknit suit carefully, taking a shower, washing out her underwear, creaming her face, brushing her hair—Jay sometimes laughed at her prolonged bedtime ritual but after all, she told him, people did get into certain habits, didn't they? And from her earliest childhood neatness had been forced upon her.

When she was ready for bed Gretchen opened the strongbox. Five thousand in cash, jewelry, title to the car, traveler's checks were in it. All her eggs shouldn't be in one basket, she told herself, and put twenty-five thousand in traveler's checks into her pocketbook.

She looked at her watch as she got into bed. Quarter of eleven and no call from Jay. She hadn't really thought there would be.

She turned out the light and was soon asleep.

The Belmont police enjoyed none of Gretchen's leisure that evening. Search of the farmhouse area, questioning of Lakeview Avenue neighbors, a return visit to Mrs. Mercer had produced nothing of value. Dr. Reilly's preliminary report told them that the bullet wound was the sole cause of death. The bullet, however, lodged in the thoracic vertabrae, had flattened out in passage and could not be used for ballistics tests.

All that the officer in charge of their own small laboratory could tell them was that it was a Smith & Wesson .32 but would fit such other guns as a Colt.

When Sergeant Tripp heard this he gave thought to the boy Mrs. Mercer had shot years ago. What was the make and caliber of the gun she used?

Only Couples Need Apply

He looked it up in the files. Webley .32 automatic pistol. She had turned it over to the police right away and asked them to get rid of it for her.

Fingerprints had been taken from the corpse and were on their way airmail to the FBI but it would be four or five days before a report on them came back.

Meanwhile, as Lieutenant Vaughan pointed out, they weren't even making any progress in establishing the Addisons' background. The most Mrs. Mercer could recall was that they had made some mention of coming from Chicago at the time she rented the apartment to them. But the Chicago police could find no record of a Jay and Gretchen Addison in telephone or city directories over the past few years. Utility companies, their business offices closed for the weekend, could not be checked immediately.

"Funny," the lieutenant said. "The two of them keeping to themselves all summer, no friends or relatives showing up at the apartment, no visitors at all, according to Mrs. Mercer. Only reference to knowing anyone in the area, she says, came just a couple of days ago when Mrs. Addison told her she was going to visit a friend in Hartford. It's like they dropped out of the sky. But they didn't. They just changed their name."

"Well, if they're wanted somewhere, maybe the FBI has Addison's prints," Yorke put in.

It was eleven o'clock. Lieutenant Vaughan, the sergeant, and Yorke, who were on the eight-to-four shift and should have gone off duty hours ago were in the lieutenant's office, talking in the flat tones of exhaustion.

"Might as well call it a night, get what sleep we can," said Vaughan. "Nothing more we can do till tomorrow."

This pronouncement came three hours too late for Yorke who'd had to break a date for tonight. The girl had complained as if it was all his fault. He had taken note of her attitude; she wouldn't make a good wife for a policeman. Not that he had any intention of getting married for years and years yet . . .

Sergeant Tripp found it easier to sit and talk about fingerprints than to get up and go home.

"No matter how good Mrs. Addison cleaned up that apartment, she would have left her prints somewhere unless she was making sure she didn't," he said. "Like she knew her husband was dead and we'd be investigating her."

"Too bad that note got handled so much there were only smudges on it," Vaughan said, not for the first time.

Tripp was on the defensive over that. How was he to know, when Mrs. Mercer handed him the note, that it offered the one chance they had of getting Gretchen Addison's prints? Besides, Mrs. Mercer had handled it plenty herself before he ever saw it . . .

"Wonder if she really was meeting a man at a motel outside of Hartford," Tripp said next. "There might be that one grain of truth in the story she gave Mrs. Mercer. Easier than making up a whole new lie."

"You think she and the man killed Addison together?" Yorke inquired.

"Who knows?" Tripp shrugged wearily and got to his feet. "All I know is, she's got a lot of questions to answer when we catch up with her."

"Maybe she's dead, too, by now," Yorke suggested. "Maybe if they were in the plot together, the man lured her somewhere and killed her."

"That sounds like a murder story on TV," said Tripp, going out the door with Lieutenant Vaughan ahead of him.

Crestfallen, Yorke followed them. Until that moment, he had been feeling pleased with himself over being in on the ground floor of the first real murder investigation—he didn't count two previous open-and-shut cases—to take place since he had joined the force.

On his way home he found solace in images of himself solving the case on his own through some brilliant stroke of reasoning that would put his name in headlines, earn him instant promotion—

He pulled his imagination up short. Promotion to what? There'd be no vacancy for a sergeant until old Halstead retired. There wasn't even the beginnings of a plainclothes division. Something came up that needed to be checked out of uniform you just took yours off and put on a suit.

But he was making some headway. No more traffic duty these days. They seemed to consider him the most promising of the younger men. And there must be occa-

Only Couples Need Apply

sions sometimes when promising young men solved cases that baffled more experienced members of a police force.

A motel outside of Hartford ...

22

But it was the New Haven police, not Yorke, who located Gretchen in the early hours of Saturday morning. Officer McBride, circling the motel parking lot on a routine check, said to his partner at the wheel, "Hey, wait a minute, something about that green Pontiac over there—"

"Stolen—on the hot sheet?"

"Don't think so. But something rings a bell from when I checked it earlier ..." McBride checked the list again. "Here it is, CKP 8950. Not stolen though." He radioed headquarters the license number, make and model of the car, waited while the computer sorted out the information that it was registered to Jay and Gretchen Addison, Belmont; that he was found shot to death yesterday morning and that Belmont police were trying to locate Gretchen Addison to notify her of his death.

"Chrissake," said the man at the wheel resignedly. "So now we've got a brand-new widow on our hands." He pulled into a vacant slot near the Pontiac. "You go in and talk to the desk clerk. He can ring her room and pave the way for us."

McBride got out and headed for the dimly lit lobby. He was gone longer than his partner anticipated and then came back and said, "More of a problem than we thought. If that's Mrs. Addison in 208, she's registered as Mrs. John Collins. Been calling the desk clerk last two or three nights asking if her husband arrived here yet."

"Oh, a cheating widow," said his partner in disgust. "Probably shacked up in there now with the other guy."

"If that's what it is, why draw attention to herself calling ahead? Simpler to just rent a room when they got here."

"Guess you're right. You didn't have the desk clerk ring her room?"

"No." McBride looked thoughtful. "Maybe we should call in and report the situation to Lieutenant Baird." He picked up the microphone and pressed the button on it. "Unit 25 calling headquarters," he said. "Over."

The dispatcher connected him with Lieutenant Baird who listened to McBride's report and said, "I'll phone the Belmont police. Stay there and keep the car under observation until I get back to you."

They waited, McBride and his partner, radio volume turned low, in the quiet darkness, the only lights visible those that ringed the parking lot.

The wait seemed long but at last their call, Unit 25, came over the radio. The lieutenant's voice crackled instructions. The Belmont police wanted to pick up Mrs. Addison themselves for questioning. Meanwhile, McBride and his partner were to keep her car under observation; another cruiser was being assigned to take over their patrol.

"If Mrs. Addison starts to leave, sir, before the Belmont police arrive, do we detain her?" McBride queried. "Over."

"Yes," the lieutenant replied. "Yes indeed."

"Yessir," said McBride. They settled down to wait.

Sergeant Tripp, grumpy and sluggish after only two hours' sleep, and Yorke, more resilient, were sent to New Haven.

It was nearly four-thirty in the morning when Yorke, who was driving, turned in at the West Rock Motel. Sergeant Tripp, wide awake now, thanked McBride and his partner for their assistance and asked them to stand by a little longer in case any question of jurisdiction came up. Then, Yorke following him, he climbed the stairway to 208.

He knocked discreetly, just a rapping of his knuckles once, twice on the door.

Gretchen heard the second rap, her sleep not that sound, more like that of some woods creature alert to danger. "Who is it?" she asked in a low voice and sat up in bed.

"Sergeant Tripp, Belmont police. Speak to you, please, about your husband."

Only Couples Need Apply

Oh God, thought Gretchen, turning on the bedside lamp.

"Just a moment," she said. She put on her robe and went to the door, trying to collect herself, already moving past the fact that a visit from the Belmont police not only was connected with Jay but that it also meant they had somehow tracked her down under the name of Mrs. John Collins.

"May I see your identification?" She kept the chain on the door as she opened it.

"Certainly." Tripp got out his folder and handed it to her through the opening.

She took her time examining it, trying to think of a story that would account for the name she was using. Movement of feet outside the door told her she was stalling to long. Suddenly she remembered what she had written in her note to Mrs. Mercer. That would do.

She handed Tripp's identification folder back to him, unfastened the chain and opened the door.

"Well?" she said, standing in the doorway.

But Tripp would have none of that. "Better if we talk inside, Mrs. Addison," he said, and edged past her with Yorke at his heels.

Their eyes swept the room. Gretchen's bed turned back where she had got out of it, the other one showing no signs of occupancy. Only her dress hanging on the recessed clothes rack, her suitcase open on the luggage stand, a strongbox on the floor beside it. No evidence of a Mr. John Collins.

"Well?" Gretchen said again as she shut the door and turned to face them.

"I'm afraid we have bad news for you, Mrs. Addison," Tripp began. "Your husband—"

"My husband? Something's happened to him—some accident? He's been gone for days . . ."

"Not exactly an accident. He's dead, though, Mrs. Addison. Shot to death."

"Oh no! Oh, my God." Gretchen leaned back against the door.

"Can I get you something, ma'am?" Yorke stepped forward. "A glass of water maybe?"

She shook her head, her eyes still fastened on Tripp as she asked, "How did it happen? Did he—kill himself?"

"No. Someone else shot him. His body was moved after death, left out in back of an old farmhouse." Tripp eyed her narrowly. If she had killed her husband herself, she was putting on a good act.

"But why?" Gretchen walked over to the nearest chair and sank down. "I can't imagine why anyone . . ."

She could, of course. Jay's money, just as she had suspected all along.

Tripp lent substance to her theory, telling her the circumstances that led to Jay's body being found, his empty wallet nearby, the Pierre Cardin shirt that had brought them to Lakeview Avenue and Mrs. Mercer.

Now she could be sure it had nothing to do with their projects, Gretchen reflected with relief. Just a matter of Jay getting drunk, getting himself robbed and murdered. It presented problems, but none, she felt, that she couldn't handle.

No mention yet of the note she had left Mrs. Mercer, who must have shown it to the police right away. Better bring it up herself . . .

Gretchen buried her face in her hands, squeezed out a few tears and raised her head to give Tripp the benefit of her emotions.

"I just can't believe it," she said helplessly. "All week I just assumed that poor Jay was off on a binge somewhere. Then last night I got a call from this man—I told Mrs. Mercer about it in the note I left her. Did she tell you?"

"Yes." Tripp sat down facing her.

"Well, I didn't go into much detail—no reason I should—but the man who called said Jay would meet me here—was already here, in fact—registered as Mr. John Collins and that I was to sign in as Mrs. John Collins . . ." Gretchen let her voice trail off, then take on a surprised note. "But how did you find me here under that name?"

"Your license number," Tripp replied briefly. "What name did this man give you?"

"Lester Morton. He said he was an old friend of Jay's, although I'd never heard Jay mention him." She gave the sergeant a wide-eyed look. "Why, he could have been the one who killed Jay!"

"It's possible. When did you say you got a call from him?"

"Last night—well, night before last, now it's almost

Only Couples Need Apply

morning." Gretchen paused. "It seems so strange, my waiting here, expecting my husband to arrive any minute and all the while he was dead, murdered—" Her voice broke as if she couldn't go on.

She still said nothing, however, Tripp noticed, about her own calls to the motel that began a night or two before the man who said his name was Lester Morton called her.

There was a lot more, it seemed, to her involved, improbable story than she intended to reveal.

Yorke, whose thoughts were following the same line, waited for the sergeant to challenge her on this point. But instead, Tripp said to him, "Call the desk and find out if a Lester Morton is registered now or if he has been any time this past week."

It came as no more of a surprise to Tripp than to Gretchen that the desk clerk said no to both questions.

Now, Yorke thought, Tripp will bring up those calls she hasn't mentioned herself.

But once again, Tripp let it go, asking instead about Tuesday evening, the last time she had seen Jay, and his past history of drinking sprees that had kept her from reporting him missing to the police.

Gretchen repeated the story she had told Mrs. Mercer, saying earnestly at the end, "Of course I never dreamed, Sergeant ..."

"How long did you intend to wait here for your husband to show up?"

"I don't know. Another day or two, I guess."

"And then?"

"Well, I suppose I would have gone back to Belmont and reported him missing," Gretchen gave Tripp her candid look as if she were speaking the truth.

She agreed the next moment to his suggestion that they start back to Belmont. She had known it would be made and had dismissed earlier thoughts of shaking them off once she was in her car, heading for the nearest bus terminal and grabbing the first bus that came along.

She would stand her ground. There would be difficult questions to face but she was already thinking ahead, preparing answers to them. The last thing in her mind, having played no part in Jay's murder, was that she might be suspected of it herself.

"We'll wait outside while you get dressed, Mrs. Addison," Tripp said, heading for the door with Yorke. When he had closed it behind them he sent Yorke down to tell their New Haven colleagues that the situation was under control and that there was no need for them to wait around any longer.

Gretchen, quick and efficient, was dressed and ready to leave in ten minutes, overnight case in one hand, strongbox and pocketbook in the other as she opened the door.

She let Yorke carry her overnight case but clung to the strongbox herself going down to her car. While she was getting out her keys Tripp put an end to any last-minute thoughts she might have had of making a break for it.

"Officer Yorke will drive you, Mrs. Addison, and I'll follow in our car," he said, and added, as she started to protest that it wasn't necessary, "Can't have you on the road alone at this hour of the morning."

He did not add that before he left himself, he intended to question the desk clerk about her calls to the motel, pinning down the dates and times as closely as possible.

Gretchen handed her keys to Yorke and got into the passenger seat beside him. His presence didn't really matter, she told herself, as he started the motor. A grieving widow couldn't be expected to make conversation during the drive. She would be almost as free as if she were alone to lapse into the silence necessary for hard thought.

She would have been chagrined over having underplayed her role if she had known that Yorke and Sergeant Tripp were both aware of what a small display of grief she had made.

23

They took her first to the hospital morgue. She barely glanced at Jay's face, nodded and turned away. Regrets over him could come later. She had herself to think about now.

Only Couples Need Apply

Mallory, the police chief, and Lieutenant Vaughan were waiting for her in Mallory's office when she arrived with her escort at nine o'clock.

They took their time beginning the interrogation, offering condolences, sending out for coffee and Danish.

Gretchen sipped her coffee, got out a cigarette murmuring thank you to Yorke who lit it for her and then, anticipating what the first question would be, said matter-of-factly, "Before we start, I'd better tell you Jay and I weren't married, just living together. But we couldn't very well tell Mrs. Mercer that, renting the apartment."

"Oh," said Vaughan, taking the lead. "What is your real name, Mrs.—uh—Addison?"

"Loomis. Miss Loomis."

Yorke, his notebook out, wrote that down.

"And your permanent address?"

Gretchen tapped ash off her cigarette. "I don't really have one, Lieutenant, not recent years. I'd been living here and there around the country until I met Jay in Chicago . . ." After a pause she continued in the same matter-of-fact tone: "Picked him up, actually, in a cocktail lounge the day I got there. He was staying at an apartment on Lake Shore Drive loaned by some friend of his and since I hadn't got a room yet, he invited me to move in with him. Which I did."

"The friend's name and address?" Vaughan inquired while Yorke waited with pen poised over notebook.

Gretchen shrugged. "Afraid I don't remember. We only stayed a few days while we looked for a place of our own."

Chicago was safe ground. No project there, no connection with the room she had taken at the YWCA before she went to Detroit.

The glances that were exchanged said this was a convenient loss of memory but no one questioned her on it, Vaughan asking instead, "You took an apartment together, Miss Loomis?"

"Yes. A furnished one at 2824 Randall Avenue." Gretchen supplied the address without hesitation. "As Mr. and Mrs. John Loomis, though, rather than in Jay's name. He was nearly a year behind in alimony payments, he said, and was afraid his ex-wife would track him down."

"Was she in Chicago too?"

"No, in Indiana somewhere. I don't know just where. Jay never said, never talked much about his past."

Gretchen spoke with growing confidence in spite of the impassive faces of her audience. She was moving along quite nicely, she felt, on what was, after all, very thin ice.

Chief Mallory asked the next question. "How long did you and Addison rent this apartment, Miss Loomis?"

She could be thankful they had kept it the whole time she was with Mrs. Engels, Jay staying on alone in the big rabbit-warren building until a week before they brought the project to its conclusion, keeping strictly to himself so that his absences to visit Gretchen in Detroit went unnoticed by other tenants.

"Oh, about six months," she replied. "I'm not very good at remembering dates but we gave it up sometime in August a year ago."

"Then where did you live before you came to Belmont in May?" Tripp put in.

This question brought her to the weakest part of her story but Gretchen met it with her shining clear-eyed look. "Well, not anywhere really, Sergeant," she said. "Or maybe I should say everywhere. Like gypsies. We'd just get in the car, pick any road that took our fancy, stop at any motel that looked right to us. We were in so many states—Kentucky, Missouri, Kansas, New Mexico, Colorado, Arizona—that they all sort of run together in my mind now." She smiled faintly. "You can see how they would."

There was no answering smile from Tripp. "But you can surely be a little more specific than that, Mrs.—uh—Miss Loomis."

She shook her head. "I'm afraid not. You can't imagine how places get mixed up in your mind when you never stay more than a week at any of them and are on the go for seven or eight months."

Their faces said they didn't believe her. Well, let them just try to prove she was lying . . .

She hurried on to firmer ground. "We drove to New York early in April—sometimes we rented cars, sometimes we flew—and stayed at the St. Regis for several weeks. I told Jay then that we had to settle down somewhere, that I'd got sick of traveling around. Jay suggested Maine for the summer and we rented a car and started

Only Couples Need Apply

out. On the way, though, I noticed the turnoff to Belmont and—"

"What name did you use at the St. Regis?" Mallory interrupted.

"Mr. and Mrs. John Loomis. But when we left, I put my foot down. I said Jay's ex-wife must have lost all track of him by that time and that I wanted us to start using his name. So then we became Mr. and Mrs. Jay Addison."

She went on to their decision to spend the summer in Belmont, the book Jay wanted to write, their looking for an apartment and answering Mrs. Mercer's ad.

"Mrs. Mercer will know just when we moved in," she said at the end. "You must realize by now, I guess, how bad I am myself at pinning down dates and places."

A short silence fell, heavy with questions still to come.

Vaughan initiated them. "Sounds like you and Addison have been flying high since you teamed up, Miss Loomis. Pretty expensive, wasn't it, neither of you working?"

"I have some money of my own, Jay seemed to have a good bit . . ." Gretchen paused, feeling that she should have a respite. "But before we go into that—and I can't see what it has to do with Jay's death—is there a women's room I could use?"

Yorke showed her the way and waited outside for her.

She was ready to assert her right to her personal privacy when she returned to Mallory's office.

"You were telling us about your income, Miss Loomis," the police chief said as soon as she was seated.

"Yes, I was, wasn't I?" Gretchen eyed him coolly. "But now that I've had a chance to think it over, I can't see what it has to do with Jay's death. Let me just say that it came from a man I lived with for some years before I ever met Jay. He was quite rich and gave me a good settlement when we broke up and he went back to his wife."

"Where was this?"

"St. Louis. But I see no reason to talk about it."

"What about Addison?" the sergeant asked. "No matter how little he told you about himself, he must have said something about where he got his money."

"He inherited it. From an uncle in Indiana, he said. I never questioned him on the details. It was his business, I felt."

"Most women would want to know more than that about it," Vaughan commented.

"If he'd wanted to tell me more, he would have," Gretchen retorted. "As a matter of fact," she added with a show of frankness, "I preferred to keep it that way. I saw no need to tell him where my money came from."

Another silence fell. Mallory and Vaughan, the senior officers present, glanced at each other. They too were on thin ice. Gretchen Addison, who now said she was Gretchen Loomis, was not under arrest, had returned to Belmont voluntarily, had answered questions freely, if not honestly, had not been warned of her constitutional rights, including her right to have a lawyer present while they questioned her. What it added up to was that they had to proceed with care themselves.

It was Vaughan who shifted ground. "Just for the record, Miss Loomis, what was your place of birth, last permanent address and so on."

"I was born in Cincinnati," Gretchen said. "After my parents died I moved around a bit until I met the man I mentioned earlier in St. Louis."

"Your age?"

"Twenty-eight."

"Ever been married?"

"No." Gretchen's tone sharpened. It was time to take the offensive. "Instead of talking about me, let's get back to Jay's death, his habit of carrying money, hundreds of dollars at a time, around with him." Her glance swept the group. "That's the answer to his murder. Someone saw it the other night. Are you checking bars he might have gone to?"

"Every bar in town," Mallory replied. "No results so far."

"I don't understand that," she said. "He didn't even have the car. I had it, going to the laundromat."

"Which one did you go to?"

"Kleen-Wash on Laurel Street." She noticed that Yorke wrote it down.

"See anyone you knew there?" Tripp inquired on a casual note. "Stay a little longer, maybe, talking to them?"

"No," Gretchen said flatly. "I brought a book along. I always do."

Tripp took a new tack. "These drinking sprees of Ad-

Only Couples Need Apply

dison's—what did you do when he went off on one during your travels together?"

"Just waited for him to come back."

"Never reported him missing?"

"No. I'd been through a couple of them in Chicago."

The questioning moved from the past to the present, their summer in Belmont, any trouble Jay might have got into, any enemies he might have made.

Presently, Chief Mallory summed up Gretchen's answers. "Seems like you had no contacts, no social life, no friends at all here in Belmont, Miss Loomis. But what about the friend you visited in Hartford the other day, the one Mrs. Mercer mentioned—what's her name?"

Gretchen looked blank for a moment. "Oh," she said. "I have no friend there. I didn't want to sit around in the apartment all day by myself, though, so I made up that story for Mrs. Mercer's benefit, just to get away and not have her fussing around."

Bitch that she was, spilling everything she knew to the police, thought Gretchen. At least there wasn't much to spill. Gretchen could thank herself, Jay not at all, for that.

To her questioners, however, with their built-in skepticism, it was just one more lie uncovered.

Only Yorke, susceptible to her good looks, still cherished a faint hope that she wasn't involved in Jay Addison's murder.

His superiors, unmoved by Gretchen's looks, shared a different view of her.

They took her back over what she had told them about her relationship with Jay. But no matter what angle they approached it from, it came out the same; and when they brought up his murder again, she still insisted that robbery was the only possible motive for it.

The second time around, Chief Mallory concluded once and for all that he didn't believe a word Gretchen said; and that among the many things she was covering up was complicity, if not actual guilt, in Addison's murder.

For the first time he mentioned the gun, listening without expression to Gretchen's disclaimer of Jay or she ever having owned one.

Oh God, she thought, why hadn't she stopped the car somewhere, anywhere yesterday and thrown it out the window? If only she hadn't been so super-cautious, wanting to get far away from Belmont before she took care of it.

But they couldn't search her car, she thought next. Weren't there all kinds of new court rulings about that sort of thing? Lacking a warrant—and they had no grounds for getting one—the gun was safe for the time being in the trunk of her car. Tonight, though, after she had signed in at a motel, she would get rid of it somehow.

It was all turning out to be much worse than she had expected. Damn Jay, anyhow, getting into some stupid mess or other that had led to his murder and put her in a spot like this. Most annoying of all was the thought that if she hadn't stayed over in New Haven last night, still hoping to hear from him, the police would never have caught up with her.

The next question came from Tripp. "The call you had night before last, Miss Loomis, from this Lester Morton—you did say you'd never heard from him before, didn't you?"

"Yes." What was he leading up to?

"And, from what you said in your note to Mrs. Mercer, he called you so late that you didn't feel you could call her to explain why you were leaving early yesterday morning."

"Yes." Gretchen eyed him warily now.

"Funny." Tripp's voice took on a reflective note. "The desk clerk told me this morning that some woman had called three or four times the past few nights asking if Mr. John Collins was registered yet. Seems to me," Tripp crossed his legs and leaned back in his chair, "that all these calls don't jibe with what you told Mrs. Mercer—and then told me."

"Oh." Gretchen took a deep breath. "Well, it was too complicated to put into a note, Sergeant, so I just condensed it. It seemed simpler to leave it like that when I talked to you. Actually, the man called me twice. The first time was Wednesday afternoon, the day after Jay disappeared. He said to keep in touch with the motel, that Jay should be there soon. That's why I called Wednesday night and Thursday night too. Then he called again very late Thursday night, said Jay had arrived there and to come yesterday morning."

Slippery as an eel, thought Tripp, and knew that his col-

Only Couples Need Apply

leagues shared his thought. Except, perhaps, Yorke, who hadn't quite got over a tendency to be taken in by a pretty face. Time—or getting married, maybe—would cure him of it.

Tripp was nearest to Gretchen's big pocketbook on the floor beside her chair. At a nod from the police chief he picked it up and carried it over to his desk.

"What are you doing, Sergeant?" Gretchen, taken by surprise, sprang to her feet. "Mr. Mallory, tell him to give it back!"

But it was already in Mallory's hands. She tried to snatch it away when she reached the desk but Tripp restrained her with a tight grip on both her arms.

"Let me go," she exclaimed, trying to shake him off. "I want a lawyer. I want one right now. You have no warrant—"

Mallory, six feet tall, loomed over her from across his desk. "Miss Loomis, you can use this phone here to call any lawyer you want to," he said. "But first let me straighten you out on one point: We can bring in a policewoman to search you without a warrant; your pocketbook is considered an extension of your person, equally open to search. Your lawyer will tell you we're within our rights examining everything in it and that there's no way you can stop us. So why not sit down and take it quietly? If you've got nothing to hide there's no need to make an issue of it."

Gretchen stared at him. He was telling the truth. She tried to hide her dismay as she went back to her chair. Uppermost in her mind were the traveler's checks in her pocketbook made out to Gretchen Slocum. She had to think of some instant explanation of it.

Slowly, deliberately, Mallory removed the contents of her pocketbook. Cosmetic case, French purse with twelve hundred dollars and a driver's license in it; no credit cards, none of the usual accumulation he would expect to find. Cigarette case, lighter, matchbooks, sunglasses, notebook, pen, facial tissues. No pictures, letters, personal papers of any sort. Everything neat, orderly and—he groped for a word—rootless.

Last of all he opened two zippered compartments bulging with folders of traveler's checks for over twenty-five thousand dollars made out to Gretchen Slocum.

He passed them on for the others' inspection. They looked at them, looked at her.

"I had them put in that name—my grandmother's maiden name—after I talked to Lester Morton," she said.

"You seem to shuffle names like a deck of cards, Miss Loomis." Vaughan made comment.

"Well, I felt I needed to take all kinds of precautions, the situation I was in," said Gretchen.

No one answered her. Mallory gathered up the contents of her pocketbook and restored it to her. "We'll have to ask you to wait, Miss Loomis, while your statement is typed up for you to sign," he said.

The implication was that she would then be free to leave. They might not believe a word she had said but they had nothing to hold her on.

Gretchen's thoughts moved ahead. Stay at a motel tonight, arrange for Jay's burial here in Belmont tomorrow, leave town right away and travel as far and as fast as she could.

Yorke took her to an empty office. He brought her another cup of coffee and the morning paper before he shut the door and left her alone.

Not really alone, though, she realized. Just outside in the main room of the police station were the officer at the desk and a man in civilian clothes typing. If she gave way to the impulse to get up and leave, they would probably stop her.

She settled back and tried to read the morning paper.

Mallory conferred with Lieutenant Vaughan and Tripp in his office, going over the evidence they had against Gretchen. Enough, they decided, to ask for a warrant to search her car.

24

Mrs. Mercer watched for the paper boy Sunday morning, anxious to find out if there was anything new on Jay Addison. There had been nothing she hadn't already known about the case in last night's news.

She brought the paper in as soon as it came and took it out to the kitchen where she had just poured herself a cup of coffee.

She couldn't believe at first the front-page headline that said WOMAN HELD IN LOVER'S SLAYING.

The story under a Belmont dateline read:

> A beautiful blonde is being held for questioning by Belmont police in the shooting death of Jay Addison, recently of Belmont. Miss Gretchen Loomis, 28, mistress of the victim, had lived here with Addison for the past several months in a Lakeview Avenue apartment owned by Mrs. Edward Mercer, lifelong Belmont resident. Addison, whose body was found Friday morning in back of a deserted farmhouse near the town line, is believed to have been killed soon after his disappearance last Tuesday evening.
>
> Miss Loomis and Addison had been posing as a married couple since their arrival in Belmont. Miss Loomis was located in a New Haven motel early yesterday morning and brought back for questioning.
>
> Belmont police and Miss Loomis's attorney, Harold E. Boyce, have refused to comment on the case. It is rumored, however, that the young woman will be charged shortly with Addison's murder.

The rest of the story was a recap of the discovery of the body, its identification by Mrs. Mercer, the search for Gretchen that had begun immediately.

It was too much to take in all at once. Mrs. Mercer stared into space, her mind blank under the impact of it.

The phone rang. It was Janet Parker. "Were you up, Anna?" she asked.

"Oh yes."

"Have you"—a pause—"seen the paper yet?"

"Yes."

"Incredible, isn't it? Who'd ever dream that such an attractive young couple, such good tenants, too, as they seemed to be, would turn out like this? And not even married, either. I'm so sorry you've been brought into it, Anna, through renting the apartment to them. Is there anything I can do to help? Would you like me to come over and keep you company?"

"No, thank you, Janet. I think I'll just get away somewhere for the day."

"Perhaps you should. There'll be reporters, I'm afraid."

Reporters. Mrs. Mercer hadn't had time yet to think about further newspaper publicity or the talk that would go on among friends and neighbors. Or that the police would probably want to question her again.

All these prospects were dwarfed by the overwhelming dilemma created by the main issue; that Gretchen Addison—no, she must began thinking of her as Gretchen Loomis—might be charged with Jay Addison's murder—and what was Mrs. Mercer going to do about that?

She would have no choice. She would have to tell the police the truth.

But not yet, she assured herself over and over while she was getting dressed, canceling a golf date, answering phone calls from friends. Not yet.

The phone rang again as she went downstairs. Not a friend this time, a reporter from Hartford asking for an interview. She said no, she had nothing to tell him. She had barely hung up when her doorbell rang. Another reporter, this one from the Belmont *Register*. She was firm in her refusal to talk to him.

When he left, Mrs. Mercer got into her car and drove out into the country, taking roads at random, crossing the state line into Massachusetts, stopping at a restaurant, suddenly aware of not having eaten all day, but discovering, when she was served, that worry and indecision robbed her of appetite.

Only Couples Need Apply 155

She still wasn't ready to go to the police, though, she realized driving home toward dark. They might let the girl go. There was no need yet for Mrs. Mercer to come forward, ruin herself.

Cowardly self-counsel, she knew; and also knew she would abide by it.

"It's no use asking me about the gun," Gretchen reiterated for—how many times?—"I don't know anything about it. I don't know how or when it got put in my wig case or who put it there."

The police chief, Vaughan and Tripp said nothing. Boyce, Gretchen's lawyer, broke the silence weighty with disbelief.

"I think we'd better drop this subject, gentlemen," he said. "Miss Loomis has told you over and over that she has no knowledge of the gun and your questions have now reached the point of harassment. I must advise her," he turned to Gretchen, "not to answer any more of them."

Goddam lawyers, thought Tripp. He went back to the jewelry but hardly listened as Gretchen repeated her statement that it had been given to her by the man in St. Louis.

It was still, that Monday afternoon, being appraised by a local jeweler.

The traveler's checks, issued by banks in Hartford and New Haven, interested Tripp far more. But Gretchen could not be budged from her assertion that her only reason for changing her name to Slocum on them was the phone call she'd had about Jay.

Boyce, getting restive as the questioning continued, finally cut it short by reminding the police officers that his client, who had been co-operating with them in every way, had now been held as a material witness for over forty-eight hours; and that if they didn't release her on bail shortly, he would apply for a writ of habeas corpus.

Gretchen listened to the discussion that went back and forth as if totally removed from it. She couldn't believe what was happening to her. She had always been so careful, so foresighted working with Jay on their projects that suspicion had never touched either of them, and yet she was now in danger of being arrested for Jay's murder, although totally innocent of it.

It couldn't be true. But it was.

She was returned to her cell. Cell! The very idea of it...

She was charged with Jay's murder that night. It was Chief Mallory's decision, with Boyce forcing his hand, not to wait, as he would have preferred to do, for the FBI report on Gretchen's fingerprints.

They had enough on her to justify the charge, Mallory said after consultation with the state's attorney. There was the gun found in her possession; the flattened bullet that killed Addison could have been fired from it. There was her hasty departure from Belmont—flight seemed a better word—with over sixty thousand in cash and traveler's checks made out in a different name. There were the lies she had told, the contradictions in every other word she spoke. There was her flat refusal to supply any information about her background—for all they knew, she still hadn't told them her real name—and, as a crowning touch, the teller in a Hartford bank who had called them late that afternoon. He had identified Gretchen from a newspaper picture as Greta Loomis who, the previous week, had closed out a joint account payable to her or John Loomis, asking for the fifteen thousand and interest in cash.

Tellers in other banks in Hartford and New Haven would now be questioned. Mallory did not doubt that other accounts under other names would be discovered.

"She killed Addison all right," he said. "Either for the money or for some reason tied in with their personal lives. The money, I'd say myself. God knows where they got it; not from any legitimate source, considering what Yorke came up with this afternoon..."

Yorke, going through Gretchen's belongings, had been struck by the incongruity of a dull-looking old book among bright new paperbacks. He couldn't have said what led him to compare it with the manuscript, supposedly the work of Jay Addison, but when he did he soon realized that the manuscript was nothing more than an updated version of the book.

It had been the cover the couple had used for hiding out all summer, Yorke's superiors said.

Gretchen said yes, Jay had plagiarized it, but intended to change it all later.

Only Couples Need Apply 157

Yorke preened himself in a modest way over his contribution to the case.

Mrs. Mercer heard on the eleven o'clock news Monday night that Gretchen had been charged with Jay Addison's murder but still made no move. She sought refuge in what the announcer had said about a grand jury indictment. They might let her go, Mrs. Mercer told herself. Or something else might come up.

But her conscience didn't let her get much sleep that night.

Tuesday afternoon the Belmont *Register* carried the story that Jay Addison's real name, traced through his fingerprints to his Army service, was Jay Hubbard; and that his place of residence at the time of his induction was Philadelphia.

"Well," Mrs. Mercer said aloud. "Well ..."

She had been steeling herself all day to call the Belmont police, holding off just in case the paper or a news report brought word of some miracle that set Gretchen free without her intervention.

Not a miracle exactly, Mrs. Mercer thought, reading the article, but at the very least another odd confusing piece of information to be added to all the other bits and pieces that made her former tenants seem more dubious by the day. So much so, that she would wait just a little longer before going to the police.

The case broke wide open Thursday. Mrs. Mercer's first knowledge of it came from the Belmont *Register* when she arrived home from a meeting that had lasted all afternoon and brought the paper in from the front porch. The headline ADDISON MURDER SUSPECT LINKED WITH OTHER KILLINGS, stunned her.

"Gretchen Loomis," she read, "charged earlier this week with the shooting death of her lover, Jay Addison, now faces additional charges in the deaths of two elderly widows in California and Florida. Both victims employed a young woman companion who vanished immediately after their murders. Among other similarities, large sums of money and valuable jewelry were missing after both murders.

"FBI ballistics tests confirm that the gun believed to have been used in the slaying of Jay Addison—whom police have now identified as Jay Hubbard, formerly of Philadelphia—took the life of Mrs. Mildred Russell of Palm Beach, Florida, early last April.

"The March 1971 murder of Mrs. Helen Atwood of Santa Barbara, California, has been linked with Miss Loomis through a set of fingerprints on file with the FBI..."

In the California murder, Mrs. Mercer read, the victim's companion was described as a stocky young woman with brown hair and brown-rimmed glasses.

The Florida victim's companion fitted the same description.

Two wigs, one brown and one black, were found among Gretchen Loomis's possessions.

Also among her possessions was a pair of antique turquoise earrings—it gave Mrs. Mercer a start to recall admiring them on Gretchen—that Mrs. Sarah Clayton of New York City, daughter of the Florida victim, had already identified as having belonged to her mother.

In both the earlier murders, the companion was believed to have had an accomplice.

Good heavens, thought Mrs. Mercer, what kind of people, what monsters, had lived in her apartment all summer and been entertained in her house?

The first time her phone rang, a friend calling to exclaim over the latest developments, Mrs. Mercer had no choice but to listen. After that she took the phone off the hook.

And presently, in a daze, started to get dinner.

The eleven o'clock news that night carried still another new development. Publicity on the national news media had brought a query from Birmingham, Michigan, police over a possible connection between the California and Florida murders and the slaying under very similar circumstances of an elderly widow, Mrs. Cora Engels, in August 1971. Mrs. Engels had employed as a companion a stockily built young woman with black hair and black-rimmed glasses. The companion had vanished on the day of her murder and money and jewelry were later discovered missing. No trace of the companion or the accomplice believed essential to the crime had ever been found.

Mrs. Mercer could take no more. She turned off the TV and made her way up to bed.